William Cobbett

Observations on the Emigration of Dr. Joseph Priestley

William Cobbett

Observations on the Emigration of Dr. Joseph Priestley

ISBN/EAN: 9783337294038

Printed in Europe, USA, Canada, Australia, Japan

Cover: Foto ©Raphael Reischuk / pixelio.de

More available books at **www.hansebooks.com**

OBSERVATIONS

ON THE

EMIGRATION

OF

Dr. JOSEPH PRIESTLEY,

AND ON THE SEVERAL ADDRESSES DELIVERED TO HIM, ON
HIS ARRIVAL AT NEW-YORK,

WITH ADDITIONS;

CONTAINING MANY CURIOUS AND INTERESTING FACTS ON
THE SUBJECT, NOT KNOWN HERE, WHEN THE
FIRST EDITION WAS PUBLISHED:

TOGETHER WITH

A COMPREHENSIVE STORY

OF A

FARMER's BULL.

———

THE *THIRD EDITION.*

" Du mensonge toujours le vrai demeure maitre :
" Pour paraitre honnête homme, en un mot, il faut l'être ;
" Et jamais, quoi qu'il faffe, un mortel ici bas,
" Ne peut aux yeux du monde être ce qu'il n'eft pas."

BOILEAU.

PHILADELPHIA:

PUBLISHED BY THOMAS BRADFORD, NO. 8, South-
Front-Street.

1795.

INTRODUCTORY ADDRESS,

To the *Gazetteers* of the City

of Philadelphia.

Gentlemen,

WHEN this Pamphlet first made its appearance in this City, you all agreed, that it might do well enough in the despotic States of Europe ; but that it was by no means fit for the meridian of the United States. And, you have very lately obliged the public with the copy of a letter from Liverpool, in which, you say, the writer observes, that the Observations on the Emigration of Doctor Joseph Priestley *have been republished* there, and that, "it is one of the most scandalous publications that ever issued from any press."
These are rather hard lines, gentlemen. I do not know what I have done, thus to draw down your vengeance on me. 'Tis true, I cannot, like you, take towns and islands as fast as Father Luke takes snuff,

or *erect a bridge acrofs the Englifh Chan-
nel with as little trouble as fome people can
the bridge of a fiddle : I cannot put Dukes
into iron cages, and fend them to Paris
for Mocking Birds, or chop away at the
heads of kings and minifters with as little
ceremony as if I were chopping a ftick of
wood : nor can I fpread fleets over the o-
cean, and religion, peace and plenty over
a country as quick as a furgeon's 'prentice
fpreads a plaifter. No, gentlemen, it is
your province to perform feats like thefe,
and, if I am not much deceived in my own
heart, I am far, very far, from envying
you your exalted ftations. But, if you are
ftrong, be merciful. 'Though you are the
great Laviathans of Literature, you may
fuffer a poor herring to fwim in the fame
fea ; there is certainly room enough for
you and me too.*

*Was it well done, gentlemen, firft to
play at foot-ball with a poor pamphlet
'till you were tired, and then turn it into
a fhuttle-cock and fet your devils to knock-
ing it from one hemifphere to the other ?
Affuredly not ; for, 'though the work itfelf might merit rough treatment at your
hands, yet. as it was in print, the natural
affection that you muft be fuppofed to bear
your typographical brethren, ought to have
'wakened in you fome compaffion towards it.*

You have had the goodnefs to inform the public, that this work is neither fit for the meridian of the United States, nor the meridian of Great Britain; but, it ap- pears that the public (in this country at leaft) think otherwife. How the public dare to differ from you in opinion I fhall not pretend to fay, but certain it is, that the numerous applications for this pam- phlet have induced me to publifh, with your leave, a third edition of it.

   To render this edition more worthy the perufal of your Honours than the laft, I have made a confiderable addition, which I have been able to do from my being now in poffeffion of fome curious facts, concern- ing the Doctor's Emigration, which were unknown on this fide the water, when the firft edition was publifhed.

   I obey the call for this edition with more pleafure, as it furnifhes me with an oppor- tunity of proving, beyond contradiction, many things, which fome people have look- ed upon as very " hazarded affertions," and which you, gentlemen (never the moft delicate) have not fcrupled to call falfhood.

   I cannot conclude this addrefs, with- out praying you to continue me your good offices. If the firft edition merit- ed your difapprobation, I am in hopes this *will be found to merit it in a much higher degree. If it should be otherwise decreed, if I am doomed to suffer your applauses, I trust, that he who is preparing me the chastisement, will give me fortitude to bear it like a man.*

I AM,

GENTLEMEN,

YOUR's, &c. &c.

THE AUTHOR.

Philadelphia
Feb. 8th. 1795.

WHEN the arrival of Doctor Priest-
ley in the United States was first announced, I
looked upon his emigration (like the propofed
retreat of Cowley, to his imaginary Paradife,
the Summer Iflands) as no more than the effect
of that weaknefs, that delufive caprice, which
too often accompanies the decline of life, and
which is apt, by a change of place, to flatter
age with a renovation of faculties, and a return
of departed genius. Viewing him as a man
that fought repofe, my heart welcomed him to
the fhores of peace, and wifhed him, what he
certainly ought to have wifhed himfelf, a quiet
obfcurity. But his anfwers to the addreffes of
the Democratic and other Societies at New-
York, place him in quite a different light, and
fubject him to the animadverfions of a public,
among whom they have been induftrioufly pro-
pagated.

No man has a right to pry into his neighbours private concerns ; and the opinions of every man are his private concerns, while he keeps them so ; that is to say, while they are confined to himself, his family and particular friends : but when he makes those opinions public ; when he once attempts to make converts, whether it be in religion, politics, or any thing else ; when he once comes forward as a candidate for public admiration, esteem or compassion, his opinions, his principles, his motives, every action of his life, public or private, become the fair subject of public discussion. On this principle, which the Doctor ought to be the last among Mankind to controvert, it is easy to perceive that these observations need no apology.

His answers to the addresses of the New-York societies are evidently calculated to mislead and deceive the people of the United States. He there endeavours to impose himself on them for a sufferer in the cause of Liberty ; and makes a canting profession of moderation, in direct contradiction to the conduct of his whole life.

He says, he hopes to find here, " that pro-" tection from violence, which laws and govern-" ment promise in all countries, but which he " has not found in his own." He certainly must suppose that no European intelligence ever reaches this side of the Atlantic, or that the inhabitants of these countries are too dull to comprehend the sublime events that mark his life and character. Perhaps I shall show him, that it is not the people of England alone who know how to eftimate the merit of Doctor Prieftley.

Let us examine his claims to our compaffion : let us fee whether his charge againft the laws and government of his country be juft, or not.

On the 14th of July, 1791, an unruly mob, affembled in the town of Birmingham, fet fire to his houfe, and burnt it, together with all it contained. This is the fubject of his complaint, and the pretended caufe of his emigration. The fact is not denied ; but in the relation of facts circumftances muft not be forgotten. To judge of the Doctor's charge againft his country, we muft take a retrofpective view of his conduct, and of the circumftances that led to the deftruction of his property.

It is about twelve years fince he began to be diftinguifhed among the diffenters from the eftablifhed church of England. He preached up a kind of *deifm*,* which nobody underftood, and which it was thought the Doctor underftood full as well as his neighbours. This doctrine afterwards affumed the name of Unitarianifm, and the *religieux* of the order were called, or rather they called themfelves, Unitarians. The fect never rofe into confequence ; and the founder had the mortification of feeing his darling Unitarianifm growing quite out of date with

---

* This is one of thofe " hazarded affertions;" alluded to in the introductory addrefs. But how is it hazarded ? The Doctor fays, in his anfwer to Paine's Age of Reafon, that " the doctrines of *atonement, incarnation*, and the " *trinity*, have no more foundation in the fcriptures, than " the doctrine of *tranfmigration*." Is not this a kind of *deifm* ? Is it not *deifm* altogether ? Can a man who denies the divinity of *Chrift*, and that he died to fave finners, have any pretenfions to the name of *Chriftian?*

himfelf, when the French Revolution came, and gave them both a fhort refpite from eternal oblivion.

Thofe who know any thing of the Englifh diffenters, know that they always introduce their political claims and projects under the mafk of religion. The Doctor was one of thofe who entertained hopes of bringing about a revolution in England upon the French plan ; and for this purpofe he found it would be very convenient for him to be at the head of a religious fect. Unitarianifm was now revived, and the fociety held regular meetings at Birmingham. In the inflammatory difcourfes, called fermons, delivered at thefe meetings, the Englifh conftitution was firft openly attacked. Here it was that the Doctor beat his drum ecclefiaftic, to raife recruits in the caufe of rebellion. The prefs foon fwarmed with publications expreffive of his principles. The revolutionifts began to form focieties all over the kingdom, between which a mode of communication was eftablifhed, in perfect conformity to that of the Jacobin Clubs in France,

Nothing was neglected by this branch of the parifian *Propagande* to excite the people to a general infurrection. Inflammatory hand-bills, advertifements, federation dinners, toafts, fermons, prayers ; in fhort, every trick that religious or political duplicity could fuggeft, was played off to deftroy a conftitution which has borne the teft, and attracted the admiration of ages ; and to eftablifh in its place a new fyftem, fabricated by themfelves.

The fourteenth of July, 1791, was of too much note in the annals of modern regeneration to be neglected by thefe regenerated politicians. A club of them, of which Doctor Prieftley was a member, gave public notice of a feaft, to be held at Birmingham, in which they intended to celebrate the French revolution. Their endeavours had hitherto excited no other fentiments, in what may be called the people of England, than thofe of contempt. The people of Birmingham, however, felt, on this occafion, a convulfive movement. They were fcandalifed at this public notice for holding in their town a feftival, to celebrate events which were in reality a fubject of the deepeft horror : and feeing in it at the fame time an open and audacious attempt to deftroy the conftitution of their country, and with it their happinefs, they thought their underftandings and loyalty infulted, and prepared to avenge themfelves by the chaftifement of the Englifh revolutionifts, in the midft of their fcandalous orgies. The feaft neverthelefs took place ; but the Doctor, knowing himfelf to be the grand projector, and confequently the particular object of his townfmen's vengeance, prudently kept away. The cry of *church and king* was the fignal for the people to affemble ; which they did to a confiderable number, oppofite the hotel where the convives were met. The club difperfed, aud the mob proceeded to breaking the windows, and other acts of violence incident to fuch fcenes ; but let it be remembered that no perfonal violence was offered. Perhaps it would have been well, if they had vented their anger on the perfons of the revolutionifts ; provided they had contented themfelves with the

ceremony of the horfe-pond or blanket. Certain it is, that it would have been very fortunate
if the riot had ended this way ; but when that
many-headed monfter, a mob, is once roufed
and put in motion, who can ftop its deftructive
fteps ?

From the *hotel of the federation* the mob proceeded to Doctor Prieftley's Meeting-Houfe, which
they very nearly deftroyed in a little time. Had
they ftopped here all would yet have been well.
The deftruction of this temple of fedition and
infidelity would have been of no great confequence ; but, unhappily for them and the town
of Birmingham, they could not be feperated, before they had deftroyed the houfes and property of many members of the club. Some of
thefe houfes, among which was Doctor Prieftley's, were fituated at the diftance of fome miles
from town ; the mob were in force to defy all
the efforts of the civil power, and, unluckily,
none of the military could be brought to the
place,. 'till fome days after the 14th of July. In
the mean time many fpacious and elegant houfes
were burnr, and much valuable property deftroyed ; but it is certainly worthy remark, that du-
ring the whole of thefe unlawful proceedings,
not a fingle perfon was killed or wounded, either
wilfully or by accident, except fome of the rioters themfelves. At the end of four or five days
this riot, which feemed to threaten more ferious
confequences, was happily terminated by the
arrival of a detachment of dragoons ; and tranquillity was reftored to the diftreffed town of
Birmingham.

The magiftrates ufed every exertion in
their power to quell this riot in its very earlieft

ſtage, and continued ſo to do to the laſt. The Earl of Plymouth condeſcended to attend, and act as a juſtice of the peace ; ſeveral clergymen of the church of England alſo attended in the ſame capacity, and all were indefatigable in their endeavors to put a ſtop to the depredations, and to re-eſtabliſh order.

Every one knows, that in ſuch caſes, it is difficult to diſcriminate, and that it is neither neceſſary nor juſt, if it be poſſible, to impriſon, try, and execute the whole of a mob, Eleven of theſe rioters were, however, indicted; ſeven of them were acquitted, four found guilty, and of theſe four, two ſuffered death. Theſe unfortunate men were, according to the law, proſecuted on the part of the king ; and it has been allowed by the Doctor's own partizans, that the proſecution was carried on with every poſſible enforcement, and even rigour, by the judges and counſellors. The pretended lenity was laid to the charge of the jury! What a contradiction! They accuſe the government of of ſcreening the rioters from the penalty due to their crimes, and at the ſame time they accuſe the jury of their acquittal ! It is the misfortune of Doctor Prieſtley and all his adherents ever to be inconſiſtent with themſelves.

After this general review of the riots, in which the Doctor was unlawfully deſpoiled of his property, let us return to the merits of his particular caſe, and his complaint; and here let it be recollected, that it is not of the rioters alone that he complains, but of the laws and government of his country alſo. Upon an examination of particulars we ſhall find, that ſo far from his having juft caufe of complaint, the laws have rendered him ftrict juftice, if not fomething more ; and that if any party has reafon to complain of their execution, it is the town of Birmingham, and not Doctor Prieftly.

Some time after the riots, the Doctor and the other Revolutionifts who had had property deftroyed, brought their actions, for damages againft the town of Birmingham, or rather againft the hundred of which that town makes a part. The Doctor laid his damages at £.4122. 11. 9. *fterling* ; of which fum £. 420. 15. o. was for works in manufcript, which he faid, had been confumed in the flames. The trial of this caufe took up nine hours : the jury gave a verdict in his favor; but curtailed the damages to £. 2502. 18. o. It was rightly confidered that the imaginary value of the manufcript works ought not to have been included in the damages ; becaufe the Doctor being the author of them, he in fact poffeffed them ftill, and the lofs could be little more than a few fheets of dirty paper. Befides if they were to be efti-mated by thofe he had publifhed for fome years before, their deftruction was a benefit inftead of a lofs, both to himfelf and his country. This fum then of £.420. 15. o. being deducted, the damages ftood at £.3701. 16. 9 ; and it fhould not be forgotten that even a great part of this fum was charged for an apparatus of phi-lofophical inftruments, which in fpite of the moft unpardonable gafconade of the Philofopher, * can be looked upon as a thing of imaginary value only ; and ought not to be estimated at its *cost* any more than a collection of shells or infects, or any other of the *frivola* of a virtuofo.

Now, it is notorious that actions for damages are always brought for much higher fums than are ever expected to be recovered. Sometimes they are brought for three times the amount of the real damage fuftained ; fometimes for double, and fometimes for only a third more than the real damage. If we view then the Doctor's eftimate in the moft favorable light, if we fuppofe that he made but the addition of one third to his real damages, the fum he ought to have received would be no more than £. 2467. 17. 10; whereas he actually received £. 2502. 18. 0; which was £. 35. 0, 2; more than he had a right to expect. And yet he complains that he has not found protection from the laws and goverment of his country ! If he had been the very beft fubject in England in place of one of the very worft, what could the laws have done more for him ? Nothing certainly can be a ftronger proof of the independence of the courts of juftice, and of the impartial execution of the laws of England than the circumftances and refult of this caufe.

---

* "You have deftroyed the moft truly valuable and ufeful "apparatus of philofophical inftruments that perhaps "any individual, in this or any other country, was ever "poffeffed of, in my ufe of which I annually fpent large "fums, with no pecuniary view whatever, but only in "the advancement of fcience, *for the benefit of my country* "*and of mankind.*"

Letter to the inhabitants of Birmingham.

A man who had for many years been the avowed and open enemy of the government and constitution, had his property destroyed by a mob, who declared themselves the friends of both, and who rose on him because he was not. This mob were pursued by the government whose cause they thought they were defending; some of them suffered death, and the inhabitants of the place where they assembled, were obliged to indemnify the man whose property they had destroyed. It would be curious to know what sort of protection this *reverend* Doctor, this "friend of humanity" wanted. Would nothing satisfy him but the blood of the whole mob? Did he wish to see the town of Birmingham, like that of Lyons, razed, and all its industrious and loyal inhabitants butchered; because some of them had been carried to commit unlawful excesses from their detestation of his wicked projects? BIRMINGHAM HAS COMBATTED AGAINST PRIESTLEY. BIRMINGHAM IS NO MORE. This I suppose would have satisfied the charitable modern philosopher, who pretended, and who the Democratic society say did, "return to his enemies blessings for curses." Woe to the wretch that is exposed to the benedictions of a modern philosopher. His "*dextre vengresse*" is ten thousand times more to be feared than the bloody poignard of the assassin: the latter is drawn on individuals only, the other is pointed at the human race. Happily for the people of Birmingham these blessings had no effect; there was no National Convention, Revolutionary Tribunal, or Guillotine, in England.

As I have already obferved, if the Doctor had been the beft and moft peaceable fubject in the kingdom, the government and laws could not have yielded him more perfect protection; his complaint, would therefore be groundlefs, if he had given no provocation to the people, if he had in nowife contributed to the riots. If then he has received ample juftice, confidered as an innocent man, and a good fubject, what fhall we think of his complaint, when we find that he was himfelf the principal caufe of thefe riots; and that the rioters did nothing that was not perfectly confonant to the principles he had for many years been labouring to infufe into their minds?

That he and his club were the caufe of the riots will not be difputed; for had they not given an infulting notice of their intention o celebrate the horrors of the fourteenth of July, accompanied with an inflammatory hand-bill, intended to excite an infurrection againft the government, * no riot would ever have taken place, and confequently its difaftrous effects would have been avoided. But, it has been faid, that there was nothing offenfive in this inflammatory hand-bill; becaufe forfooth "the "matter of it (however indecent and untrue) "was not *more virulent* than Paine's Rights of "man, Mackintofh's anfwer to Burke, Remarks

---

* This hand-bill was difowned by the club, and they offered a reward for apprehending the author; but they took care to fend him to France before their advertifement appeared.

" on the conftitution of England,&c. &c. which
" had been lately publifhed without incurring the
"*cenfure of government*." So; an inflammatory
performance, acknowledged to be *indecent* and
untrue, is not offenfive, becaufes it is not *more
virulent* than fome other performances, which
have efcaped the cenfure of government! If this
is not a new manner of arguing, it is at leaft an
odd one. But this hand-bill had fomething
more malicious in it, if not *more virulent*, than
even the inflammatory works above mentioned.
They were more difficult to come at; to have
them they muft be bought. *They* contained
fomething like reafoning, the fallacy of which
the government was very fure would be detect-
ed, by the good fenfe of thofe who took the
pains to read ,them. A hand-bill was a more
commodious inftrument of fedition : It was
calculated to have immediate effect. Befides, if
there had been nothing offenfive in it, why did
the club think proper to difown it in fo ceremo-
nious a manner ? They difowned it with the
moft folemn affeverations, offered a reward for
apprehending the author, and afterwards jufti-
fied it as an inoffenfive thing. Here is a palpa-
ble inconfiftency. The fact is, they perceived
that this precious morfel of eloquence, in place
of raifing a mob for them, was like to raife one
againft them : they faw the ftorm gathering,
and in the moment of fear difowned the writing. After the danger was over, feeing they
could not exculpate themfelves from the charge
of having publifhed it, they defended it as an
inoffenfive performance.

The Doctor, in his juſtiſicatory letter to the people of Birmingham, ſays that the company were aſſembled on this occaſion " to celebrate " the emancipation of a neighbouring nation from " tyranny, without intimating a deſire of *any thing* "*more* than *an improvement of their own conſtitution.*" Exceſſive modeſty ! *Nothing but an improvement ?* A la françoise of courſe ? However with reſ-pect to the church, as it was a point of con-ſcience, the club do not ſeem to have been altoge-ther ſo moderate in their deſigns. " Believe me," ſays the Doctor, in the ſame letter, " the church " of England, which you think you are ſupport-"ing, has received a greater *blow* by this conduct " of yours than *I* and *all my friends* have ever *aim-*" *ed at it.*" They had then it ſeems aimed *a blow* at the eſtabliſhed church, and were forming a plan for *improving* the conſtitution ; and yet the Doctor, in the ſame letter, twice expreſſes his aſtoniſhment at their being treated as the ene-mies of church and ſtate. In a letter to the ſtudents of the college of Hackney he ſays, a "Hierarchy, equally *the bane of chriſtianity and ra-*" *tional liberty*, now confeſſes its weakneſs ; and "be aſſured that you will ſee its complete reforma-" tion or *its fall.*" And yet he has, the aſſurance to tell the people of Birmingham, that their ſuperiors have deceived them in repreſent-ing him and his ſect as the enemies of church and ſtate.

But, ſay they, we certainly exerciſed the right of freemen in aſſembling together ; and even if our meeting had been unlawful, cogniz-ance ſhould have been taken of it by the ma-

giſtracy : there can be no liberty where a ferocious mob is ſuffered to ſuperſede the law. Very true. This is what the Doctor has been
told a thouſand times, but he never would believe it. He ſtill continued to bawl out : " The
" ſunſhine of reaſon will aſſuredly chaſe away and
" diſſipate the miſts of darkneſs and error ; and
" when the majeſty of the people *is inſulted*, or
" they feel themſelves oppreſſed by *any ſet of*
" *men*, they have the power to redreſs the griev-
" ance." So the people of Birmingham, feel-
ing their majeſty inſulted by *a ſet of men* (and
a very impudent ſet of men too), who audaci-
ouſly attempted to perſuade them that they were
" *all ſlaves and idolaters*," and to ſeduce them
from their duty to god and their country, roſe
" *to redreſs the grievance*." And yet he complains ? Ah ! ſays he, but, my good townſmen,
    " ————you miſtake the matter :
    " For, in all ſcruples of this nature,
    " No man includes *himſelf* nor turns
    " the point upon his own concerns."
And therefore he ſays to the people of Birmingham : " You have been miſled." But
had they ſuffered themſelves to be miſled by
himſelf into an inſurrection againſt the government ; had they burnt the churches, cut the
throats of the clergy, and hung the magiſtrates,
military officers and nobility to the lamp poſts,
would he not have ſaid that they exerciſed a
ſacred right ? Nay, was not the very feſtival,
which was the immediate cauſe of the riots, held
expreſsly to celebrate ſcenes like theſe ? to celebrate the inglorious triumphs of a mob ? The
fourteenth of July was a day marked with the

blood of the innocent, and eventually the deftruction of an empire. The events of that day muft
ftrike horror to every heart except that of a de-
iftical philofophei, and would brand with eternal infamy any other nation but France ; which
thanks to the benign influence of the Rights of
Man, has made fuch a progrefs in ferociouf-
nefs, murder, facrilege, and every fpecies of infamy, that the horrors of the fourteenth of July
are already forgotten.

What we celebrate we muft approve ; and
does not the man, who approved of the events
of the fourteenth of July, blufh to complain of
the Birmingham riots ? " Happily," fays he to
the people of Birmingham, "happily the minds
" of Englifhmen have a horror for *murder*, and
" therefore you did not, I hope, think of that;
" though by your clamourous demanding me at
" at the hotel, it is probable that, at that time,
" fome of you intended me fome perfonal inju-
" ry." Yes, Sir, happily the minds of Englifhmen have a horror for murder ; but who will
fay that the minds of Englifhmen, or Englifh
women either would have a horror for murder,
if you had fucceeded in overturning their religion and conftitution, and introducing your
Frenchified fyftem of liberty ? The French were
acknowledged to be the moft polite, gentle,
compaffionate and hofpitable people in all Europe : what are they now ? Let Lafayette, Brif-
fot, Anacharfis Cloots, or Thomas Payne himfelf anfwer this queftion.

Let us fee a little how mobs have acted under the famous goverment that the Doctor fo
much admires.

I shall not attempt a detail of the horrors committed by the cut-throat Jourdan and his associates in Provence, Avignon, Languedoc, and Roussillon. Towns and villages sacked, gentlemen's seats and castles burnt, and their inhabitants massacred; magistrates insulted, beat, and imprisoned, sometimes killed; prisoners set at liberty to cut the throats of those they had already robbed. The exploits of this band of *patriots* would fill whole volumes. They reduced a great part of the inhabitants of the finest and most fertile country in the whole world, to a degree of misery and ruin that would never have been forgotten, had it not been so far eclipsed since, by the operation of what is, in "that devoted country," called the the law. The amount of the damages sustained in property, was perhaps a hundred thousand times as great as that sustained by the Revolutionists at Birmingham. When repeated accounts of these murderous scenes were laid before the National Assembly, what was the consequence? what the redress? "We had our fears" said Monsieur Gentil, "for the prisoners of Avignon, and for " the lives and property of the inhabitants of "that unhappy country; but these fears are now " changed into a certainty : the prisoners are " released; the country feats are burnt,and" ----- Monsieur Gentil was called to order, and not suffered to proceed; after which these precious "Guardians of the Rights of Man" passed a censure on him, for having slandered the patriots. It is notorious that the chief of these cutthroats, Jourdan, has since produced his butcheries in Avignon as a proof of his *civism*, and that he is now a diftinguifhed charaƈter among the real friends of the Revolution.

Does the Doƈtor remember having heard any thing about the glorious atchievements of the 10th of Auguft, 1792? Has he ever made an eftimate of the property deftroyed in Paris on that and the follcwing days? Let him compare the deftruƈtion that followed the fteps of that mob, with the lofs of his toafted apparatus ; and when he has done this, let him tell us, if he can, where he would now be, if the government of England had treated him and friends, as the National Affembly did the fufferers in the riots of the 10th of Auguft. But, perhaps, he looks upon the events of that day as a glorious victory, a new emancipation, and of courfe will fay, that I degrade the *Herocs* in calling them a mob. I am not for difputing with him about a name ; he may call them the heroes of the 10th of Auguft, if he will : " The Heroes of the 14th of July," has always been underftood to mean, *a gang of blood thirfty cannibals*, and I would by no means wifh to withold the title from thofe of the 10th of Auguft.

Will the Doƈtor allow, that it was a mob that murdered the ftate prifoners from Orleans? or does he infift upon calling that maffacre an *aƈt of civifm*, and the aƈtors in it, the heroes of the 12th of September ? But whether it was an aƈt of civifm, a maffacre or a victory, or whatever it was, I cannot help giving it a place here, as I find it recorded by his countryman, Doƈtor Moore. " The mangled todies," fays he, " were lying " in the ftreet on the left hand as you go to the. " *Chateau* from Paris. Some of the lower fort of

" the inhabitants of Verſailles were looking on;
" the reſt ſtruck with terror, were ſhut up in their
" ſhops and houſes. The body of the Duke of
" Briſſac was pointed out, the head and one of
" the hands was cut off! a man ſtood near
" ſmoking tobacco, with his ſword drawn, and
" a human hand ſtuck on the point! another
" fellow walked careleſly among the bodies
" with an entire arm of another of the priſoners
" fixed to the point, of his ſword! A waggon
" afterwards arrived, into which were thrown
" as many of the ſlaughtered bodies as the
" horſes could draw! a boy of about fifteen
" years of age was in the waggon, aſſiſting to
" receive the bodies as they were put in, and
" packing them in the moſt convenient manner,
" with an air of as much indifference as if they
" had been ſo many parcels of goods! One of
" the wretches who threw in the bodies, and
" who probably had aſſiſted in the maſſacre,
" ſaid to the ſpectators in praiſe of the boy's ac-
" tivity ; " See that little fellow there ; how bold
" he is ! ""

" The aſſaſſins of the priſoners were a party
" who came from Paris the preceding evening,
" moſt of them in poſt chaiſes, for that purpoſe,
" and who attacked thoſe unhappy men while
" they remained in the ſtreet, waiting 'till the
" gate of the priſon which was prepared for
" their reception, ſhould be opened. The detach-
" ment which had guarded the priſoners from
" Orleans, ſtood ſhameful and paſſive ſpectators
" of the maſſacre,—The miſerable priſoners be-
" ing all unarmed, and ſome of them fettered,
" could do nothing in their own defence : they

" were moſt of them ſtabbed--and a few, who at-
" tempted reſiſtance, were cut down with ſabres.
" There never was a more barbarous and
" daſtardly action performed in the face of the
" ſun.—Gracious Heaven! Were thoſe barbari-
" ties, which would diſgrace ſavages, committed
" by Frenchmen! by that lively and ingenu-
" ous people, whoſe writings were ſo much ad-
" mired, whoſe ſociety has been ſo much cour-
" ted, and whoſe manners have been ſo much
" imitated by all the neighbouring nations?—
" This attrocious deed, executed in the ſtreets
" of Verſailles, and the horrors committed in
" the priſons of Paris, will fix indelible ſtains
" on the character of the French nation. It is
" ſaid thoſe barbarities revolted the hearts of
" many of the citizens of Paris and Verſailles,
" as much as they could thoſe of the inhabitants
" of London or Windſor. It is alſo ſaid that
" thoſe maſſacres were not committed by the
" inhabitants of Paris or Verſailles, but by a
" ſet of hired aſſaſſins.—But who hired thoſe
" aſſaſſins? Who remained in ſhameful ſtupor
" and daſtardly inactivity, while their laws
" were inſulted, their priſons violated, and
" their fellow citizens butchered in the open
" ſtreets? I do not believe, that from the
" wickedeſt gangs of highway-men, houſe-
" breakers, and pick-pockets, that infeſt Lon-
" don and the neighbourhood, men could be
" ſelected who could be bribed to murder in
" cold blood, ſuch a number of their country-
" men!—and if they could, I am convinced
" that no degree of popular deluſion they are ca-

D

" pable of, no pretext, no motive whatever,
" could make the inhabitants of London or
" Windfor, or any town of Great Britain, fuffer
" fuch dreadful executions to be performed
" within their walls."

No ; I hope not : yet I do not know what
might have been effected, by an introduction
of the fame fyftem of anarchy, that has changed the airy amiable French into a fet of the
moft ferocious inhuman blood-hounds, that ever
difgraced the human fhape.

From fcenes like thefe, the mind turns for relief and confolation to the riot at Birmingham.
That riot confidered comparatively with what
Doctor Prieftley and his friends wifhed and attempted to ftir up, was peace, harmony and
gentlenefs. Has this man any reafon to complain ? He will perhaps fay, he did not approve
of the French riots and maffacres ; to which I
fhall anfwer, that he did approve of them. His
public celebration of them was a convincing
proof of this ; and if it were not, his fending his
fon to Paris, in the midft of them, to requeft the
honour of becoming a French citizen, is a proof
that certainly will not be difputed.* If then we

* Another " hazarded affertion." Let us hear the Doctor again. " My fecond Son, who was prefent both at the
" riot, and the affizes, felt more indignation ftill. and wil-
" lingly liftened to a propofal to fettle in France ; and
" there his reception was but too flattering." It is ufelefs
to afcertain the time of this flattering reception, in order to
prove that it was in the midft of maffacres · for the revolution has been one continued fcene of murder and rapine ;
but, however, if the reader has an opportunity of examining
the Paris papers, he will find that the ceremony took place
within a very few days of the time when Jourdan filled
the *Ice-houfe* at Avignon with mangled bodies.

take a view of the riots of which the doctor is an admirer, and of those of which he expresses his detestation, we must fear that he is very far from being that " *friend of human happiness*," that the democratic society pretend to believe him. In short, in whatever light we view the Birmingham riots, we can see no object that excites our compassion, except the inhabitants of the Hundred and the unfortunate Rioters themselves.

The charge that the Doctor brings against his country is, that it has not *afforded him protection*. It ought to be remarked here, that there is a material difference between a government that does not at all times afford *sufficient protection*, and one that is *oppressive*. However, in his answer to the New-York addresses, he very politely acquiesces in the government and laws of England being oppressive also. Would he really prefer the proceedings of a *revolutionary Tribunal* to those of a court of justice in England? Does he envy the lot of his colleagues Manuel, Lacroix, Danton and Chabot? How would he look before a tribunal like that of the Princess de Lambelle, for example? When this much lamented unfortunate lady was dragged before the villains that sat in a kind of mock judgment on her, they were drinking *eau de vie*, to the damnation of those that lay dead before them. Their shirt sleeves were tucked up to their elbows their arms and hands, and even the goblets they were drinking out of, were besmeared with human blood! I much question if the assassin's stab, or even the last pang of death with all its concomitant bitterness, was

half fo terrible as the blood-freezing fight of
thefe hell-hounds. Yet this was a *court of juftice*, under that conftitution which " the friend
" of human happinefs" wanted to impofe on
his countrymen ! Paine in fpeaking of the Englifh government, fays exultingly, and as he
fancies wittily : " they manage thofe things bet-
"ter in France." I fancy, this boafting "reprefenta-
" tive of twenty four millions of free men" would
now be glad to exchange his poft of deputy for
that of under fhoe black to the meaneft Laquay
at the court of London ! Would he not with joy
exchange his *cachot* with the reverfion of the
guillotine into the bargain, for the darkeft cell
in that very Baftile, the deftruction of which
he has fo triumphantly and heroically fung ? His
fate is a good hint to thofe who change countries
every time they crofs the fea. A man of all
countries is a man of no country : and let all
thofe citizens of the world remember, that he
who has been a bad fubject in his own country,
though from fome latent motive he may be well
received in another, will never be either *trufted*
or *refpected*.

The Doctor and his fellow labourers who
have lately emigrated to Botany Bay, have been
continually crying out : " a reform of Parliament." The fame vifionary delufion feems to have
pervaded all reformers in all ages. They do not
confider what *can* be done, but what they think
ought to be done. They have no calculating
principle to direct them to difcover whether a reform will coft them more than it is worth or not.
They do not fit down to count the coft ; but,
the object being, as they think, defirable, the

means are totally difregarded. If the French reformers had fit down to count the coft, I do not
believe they were villains or ideots enough to have
purfued their plan as they did. To fave a tenth
part of their income, they have given the whole,
or rather it has been taken from them. To
preferve the life of a perfon now and then unjuftly condemned, they have drenched the country
with the blood of the innocent. Even the Baftile,
that terrible monument of tyranny, which has
been painted in fuch frightful colours, contained
but *two* ftate prifoners when it was forced by the
mob ; and the reformers to deliver thefe two
prifoners, and to guard others from a like fate,
have erected Baftiles in every town and in every
ftreet. Before the Revolution there were only
two ftate prifoners, there are now above *two
hundred thoufand.* Do thefe people calculate ?
Certainly not. They will not take man as
they find him, and govern him upon principles
eftablifhed by experience ; they will have him
to be " a faultlefs monfter that the world ne'er
faw," and wifh to govern him according to a
fyftem that never was, or can be, brought into
practice.

Thefe waking dreams would be of no more
confequence than thofe of the night, were they
not generally purfued with an unjuftifiable degree of obftinacy and intrigue, and even villainy;
and did they not, being always adapted to flatter and inflame the lower orders of the people,
often baffle every effort of legal power. Thus
it happened in England in the reign of Charles
the firft ; and thus has it happened in France.
Some trifling innovation always paves the way

to the fubverfion of a government. The ax in
the foreft humbly befought a little piece of wood
to make it a handle : the foreft confifting of fo
many ftately trees, could not, without manifeft
cruelty, refufe the " humble " requeft ; but,
the handle once granted, the before-contemptible
tool began to lay about it with fo much violence,
that in a little time not a tree nor even fhrub
was ftanding. That a parliamentary reform
was the handle by which the Englifh revolutionifts intended to effect the deftruction of the conftitution needs not be infifted on ; at leaft if we
believe their own repeated declarations. Paine
and fome others clearly expreffed themfelves on
this head : the Doctor was more cautious while
in England, but, fafely arrived in his " afylum,"
he has been a little more undifguifed. He fays
the troubles in Europe are the natural offspring
of the " *forms of government*" that exift there ;
and that the abufes fpring from the " *artificial
diftinctions in fociety.*"—I muft ftop here a moment to remark on the impudence of this affertion. Is it not notorious that *changing* thofe
forms of government, and *deftroying* thofe diftinctions in fociety, has introduced all the troubles
in Europe ? Had the form of government in
France continued what it had been for twelve or
thirteen hundred years, would thofe troubles ever
have had an exiftence. To hazard an affertion
like this, a man muft be an idiot, or he muft think
his readers fo.—It was then the *form* of the Englifh government, and thofe artificial diftinctions ; that is to fay, of king, prince, bifhop, &c.
that he wanted to deftroy, in order to produce
that " *other fyftem of liberty,*" which he had been

fo long dreaming about. In his anfwer to the addrefs of " the republican natives of Great Bri- " tain and Ireland, refident at New-York," he fays : " the wifdom and happinefs of republican " governments, and the evils refulting from " hereditary monarchial ones, cannot appear in " a ftronger light to you than they do to me ;" and yet this fame man pretended an inviolable attachment to the *hereditary monarchial govern- ment* of Great Britain ! Says he, by way of vin- dicating the principles of his club to the people of Birmingham " the firft toaft that was drunk, was, " *the king and conftitution.*" What ! does he make a merit in England of having *toafted* that which he abominates in America ? Alas ! Philo- fophers are but mere men !

It is clear that a parliamentary reform was not the objeƈt : an after game was intended, which the vigilance of government, and the natural good fenfe of the people happily pre- vented ; and the Doƈtor, difappointed and cha- grined, is come here to difcharge his heart of the venom it has been long collecting againft his country. He tells the Democratic fociety that he cannot promife to be a better fubjeƈt of this government than he has been of that of Great Britain. Let us hope that he intends us an agreeable difappointment, if not, the fooner he emigrates back again the better.

Syftem mongers are an unreafonable fpecies of mortals : time, place, climate, nature itfelf muft give way. They muft have the fame go- vernment in every quarter of the globe ; when perhaps there are not two countries which can poffibly admit of the fame form of government, at

the fame time. A thoufand hidden caufes, a
thoufand circumftances and unforefeen events
confpire to the forming of a government. It is
always done by little and little. When com-
pleated, it prefents nothing like a *fyftem*; nothing
like a thing compofed, and written in a book.
It is curious to hear people cite the American
government as the fummit of human perfection
while they decry the Englifh; when it is abfo-
lutely nothing more than the government which
the kings of England eftablifhed here, with fuch
little modifications as were neceffary on account
of the ftate of fociety and local circumftances.
If then the Doctor is come here for a change of
government and laws, he is the moft difappointed
of mortals. He will have the mortification to
find in his "*afylum*" the fame laws as thofe from
which he has fled, the fame upright manner of
adminiftering them, the fame punifhment of the
oppreffor and the fame protection of the op-
preffed. In the courts of juftice he will every
day fee precedents quoted from the Englifh law-
books; and (which to him may appear wonderful) we may venture to predict, that it will
be very long before they will be fupplanted by
the bloody records of the revolutionary tribunal.
Let him compare the governments of thefe ftates,
and the meafures they have purfued, with what
has paffed under the boafted conftitution that
he wifhed to introduce into England, and fee if
he can find one fingle inftance of the moft
diftant refemblance. In the abolition of negro
flavery for example, the governments of the United States have not rufhed headlong into the
mad plan of the National Convention. With
much more humane views; with a much more

fincere defire of feeing all mankind free and happy, they have, in fpite of clubs and focieties, proceeded with caution and juftice. In fhort, they have adopted, as nearly as poffible, confidering circumftances and fituation, the fame meafures as have been taken by the government which he abhors. He will have the further mortification to find, that the government here is not, any more than in England, influenced by the vociferations of fifh-women, or by the *toafts* and *refolutions* of popular focieties. He will, however, have one confolation, here as well as there, he will find, that the truly great, virtueus and incorruptible man at the head of government, is branded for an *Ariftocrat*, by thofe noify gentry.

Happinefs being the end of all good government, that which produces the moft is confequently the beft; and comparifon being the only method of determining the relative value of things, it is eafy to fee which is preferable, the tyranny which the French formerly enjoyed, or the liberty and equality they at prefent labour under. If the Doctor had come about a year fooner, he might have had the fatisfaction of being not only an ear, but an eye-witnefs alfo, of fome of the bleffed effects of this celebrated revolution. He might then have been regaled with that fight, fo delectable to a modern philofoper;—opulence reduced to mifery.

The ftale pretence, that the league againft the French has been the caufe of their inhuman conduct to each other, cannot, by the moft perverfe fophiftry, be applied to the Ifland of St.

E

Domingo. That fine rich colony was ruined, its superb capital and villas reduced to aſhes, one half of its inhabitants maſſacred, and the other half reduced to beggary, before an enemy ever appeared on the coaſt. No: it is that ſyſtem of anarchy and blood that was celebrated at Birmingham on the 14th of July, 1791, that has been the cauſe of all this murder and devaſtation.

Nor let the Doctor pretend that this could not be foreſeen. It was foreſeen and foretold too, from the very moment a part of the Deputies to the States General were permitted to call themſelves a national aſſembly. In proof of this, I could mention a dozen publications that came out under his own eye; but I ſhall content myſelf with giving a ſhort extract from a ſpeech in the Britiſh parliament, which is the more proper on this occaſion, as it was delivered but a few weeks before the period of theriots. " The Americans," ſaid Mr. Burke, " have
" what was eſſentially neceſſary for freedom ;
" they have the phlegm of the good tempered
" Engliſhmen——they were fitted for Republi-
" cans by a republican education. Their revo-
" lution was not brought about by baſe and dege-
" nerate crimes; nor did they overturn a govern-
" ment for the purpoſes of anarchy; but they raiſ-
" ed a republic, as nearly repreſenting the Britiſh
" government as it was poſſible. They did not
" run into the abſurdity of France, and by ſeiz-
" ing on the *rights of man*, declare that the
" nation was to govern the nation, and Prince

" Prettyman to govern Prince Prettyman.*
" There are in Canada many of the ancient inha-
" bitants; will it be proper to give them the
" French conſtitution? In my opinion there
" is not a ſingle circumſtance that recommends
" the adoption of any part of it, for the whole
" is abominably bad—the production of folly
" not wiſdom— of vice, not virtue; it contains
" nothing but extremes, as diſtant from each
" as the poles—the parts are in eternal oppo-
" ſition to each other—it is founded on what
" is called the *rights* of man, but to my convic-
" tion it is founded on the *wrongs* of man, and
" I now hold in my hand an example of its ef-
" fects on the French colonies—Domingo,
" Guadaloupe, and the other French Iſlands,
" were rich, happy, and growing in ſtrength
" and conſequence in ſpite of the three laſt
" diſtreſſing wars, before they heard of the
" new doctrine of the rights of man ; but theſe
" rights were no ſooner arrived at the Iſlands,
" than any ſpectator would have imagined that
" Pandora's box had been opened, and that Hell
" had yawned out diſcord, murder, and every
" miſchief; for anarchy, confuſion and blood-
" ſhed raged every where ; it was a general
" ſummons for

---

* If this gentleman could ſee *a raxt* publiſhed a few
days ago, by *my old friends*, the New York Democratic Society, he would find that we are improved;
and that Prince Prettyman is to govern Prince
Prettyman here as well as in France. "What" ſay they,
" ſhall preſerve public liberty, but the wiſdom of an 'en-
" lightened people? In every free ſtate the ſovereignty
" is veſted in the people, and every individual is at once
" *a legiſlator* and *a ſovereign*."

    " Black fpirits, and white,
    " Blue fpirits, and grey,
    " Mingle, mingle, mingle,
    " You that mingle may."
" When the affembly heard of thefe diforders,
" they ordered troops to quell them ; but it
" proves that the troops have joined the infur-
" gents, and murdered their commander. I
" look on the revolution with horror and detef-
" tation ; it is a revolution of confummate folly,
" formed and maintained by every vice."

But perhaps the Doctor's intenfe ftudies ; "his
" continual labours for the good of mankind,"
might not leave him time to perufe the debates
of parliament ; however, we may fairly pre-
fume that he read the letters addreffed to himfelf ; and if fo, he has read the following paffage , " you think that a neighbouring nation
" is emancipated from tyranny, and that a com-
" pany of Englifhmen may laudably exprefs
" their joy on the occafion. Were your premi-
" fes true, I would allow your conclufion. But
" let us wait the event. Philofophers fhould
" not be too credulous, or form their determi-
" nations too rafhly. It is very poffible that
" all the magnificent fchemes of your auguft
" diet in France may be fucceeded by a ridicu-
" lous, a villainous, or a bloody cataftrophe."

Either he forefaw the confequences of the
French Revolution or he did not forefee them :
if he did not, he muft confefs that his penetra-
tion was far inferior to that of his antagonifts,
and even to that of the multitude of his countrymen ; for they all forefaw them. If he did
forefee them, he ought to blufh at being called

the " friend of human happiness ;" for, to fore-
see such dreadful calamities and to form a delibe-
rate plan for bringing them upon his country he
muft have a difpofition truely diabolical. If he
did not forefee them, he muft have an under-
ftanding little fuperior to that of an idiot ; if he
did, he muft have the heart of a *Marat*. Let
him choofe.

But it is pretty clear that he forefaw the confequences, or, at leaft, that he approves of
them ; for, as I have obferved above, he fent his
fon into France, in the very midft of the maffacres, to requeft the honor of becoming a
French citizen ; and in his anfwer to the addreffers at New York, he takes good care to exprefs
his difaprobation of the war purfued by his country (which he calls an infatuation) becaufe its
manifeft tendency is to deftroy that hydra, that
fyftem of anarchy which is the primary caufe.
Befides, is not his emigration itfelf a convincing
proof, that his opinion ftill remains the fame ?
If he found himfelf miftaken, he would confefs
his error ; at leaft tacitly, by a change of conduct. Has he done this ? No : the French revolution is his fyftem, and fooner than not fee
it eftablifhed, I much queftion if he would not
with pleafure fee the maffacre of all the human
race.

Even fuppofe his intended plan of improvement had been the beft in the world inftead of
the worft : the people of England had certainly
a right to reject it. He claims, as an indubita-
ble right, the right of thinking for *others*, and
yet he will not permit the people of England to
think for *themfelves*. Paine fays : " what a

whole nation *wills*, it has a right *to do*." Confequently, what a whole nation does *not will*, it
has a right *not to do*. Rouffeau fays : " the majority of a people has a right to *force* the reft to
be *free* ;" but even the " infane Socrates of the
national affembly" has never, in all his abfurd
reveries, had the folly to pretend, that a club
of diffenting malcontents has a right to *force* a
whole nation to be *free*. If the Englifh chofe
to remain flaves, bigots, and idolators, as the
Doctor calls them, that was no bufinefs of his :
he had nothing to do with them. He fhould
have let them alone ; and perhaps in due time,
the abufes of their government would have come
to that " *natural termination*," which he trufts
" will guard againft future abufes." But, no,
faid the Doctor, I will reform you, —I will en-
lighten you, —I will will make you free. You
fhall not ! fay the people. But I will ! fays the
Doctor. By ——, fay the people, you fhall not !
" *And when* Ahithopel *faw that his counfel was*
" *not followed, he faddled his afs, and arofe, and*
" *gat him home to his houfe, to his city, and put his*
" *houfehold in order, and hanged himfelf, and*
" *died and was buried in the fepulchre of his*
" *father.*"
I now beg the reader's company in a flight review of the addreffes, delivered to the Doctor by
the feveral patriotic focieties at New York. *

* I. An addrefs from " th *Democratic Society* "
II. From the " *Tammany Society*."
III. From the " *Affociated Teachers*."
IIII, From the " *Republican Natives of Great Britain*
" *and Ireland*."
Thofe addreffes, with the anfwers to them, having all
appeared in the Gazettes, it will be ufelefs to give
them at length here.

: It is no more than juſtice to ſay of theſe ad-
dreſſes, in the lump, that they are diſtinguiſhed
for a certain barrenneſs of thought and vulgarity
of ſtyle, which, were we not in poſſeſſion of the
Doctor's anſwers, might be thought inimitable.
If the parties were leſs known, one might be
tempted to think that the addreſſers were dull
by concert; and that by way of retaliation, the
Doctor was reſolved to be as dull as they. At
leaſt, if this was their deſign, nobody will deny
but they have ſucceeded to admiration.

"The governments of the old world," ſay the
Democratic Soicety, " are moſt of them now
" baſely combined to prevent the eſtabliſhment
" of liberty in France, and to effect the total
" deſtruction of the rights of man."

What! The Rights of Man yet? I thought
that *Liberty and Equality, the Rights of Man,*
and all that kind of political cant, had long been
diſcovered for the greateſt Bore in nature.
Are there people in this country, and people
who pretend to poſſeſs a ſuperior degree of ſa-
gacity too, who are dolts enough to talk about
French Liberty, after what paſſes under their eyes
every day? Is not every Frenchman in the
United States, obliged to go to a juſtice of the
peace, every two or three months, to have a
certificate of reſidence? And muſt he not have
this certificate ſworn to and ſigned, by four inhabitants beſides the magiſtrate? And muſt
he not pay for this too? And if he fails in
any part of this ſlaviſh ceremony, or goes into
Canada or Florida, is he not marked out for the
Guilliotine? An Engliſhman may come when
he will, ſtay as long as he pleaſes, go where he

will, and return when he will to his own country, without finding any law of profcription, or
confifcation, iffued againſt him or his property.
Which has moſt liberty?

I thought no one would dun our ears with
French liberty, after the decree which obliges every merchant, under pain of the Guilliotine, to
make a declaration of all his property in foreign
countries, and to give up his right and title of
fuch property to the convention; and not only
to make a declaration of his own, but of his
neighbour's property alfo, under the fame penalty! It has long been cuſtomary to exprefs a
deteſtation of the tyranny and cruelty of the Inquifition: but the Inquifition, in the height of
its feverity, was never half fo tyrannical as this
decree. This is the boaſted "gallic liberty."
Let us hear their own definition of this liberty.
" Liberty," fays Barrere, in his report to the
National Convention, on the 3d of January 1794,
" Liberty, my dear fellow citizens, is a privi-
" ledged and general creditor; not only has
" ſhe a right to our *property* and *perfons*, but to
" our *talents* and *courage*, and even to our
" *thoughts*!" Oh Liberty! What a metamor-
phoſis haſt thou undergone in the hands of thefe
political juglers!

If this be liberty, may God in his mercy continue me the moſt abject flave. If this be liberty, who will fay that the Engliſh did not do well
in rejecting the Doctor's plan for making them
free? The Democrats of New York, accufe the
allies of being combined to prevent the eſtabliſhment of liberty in France, and to deſtroy the
rights of man; when it is notorious that the

French themfelves have banifhed the very idea of the thing from amongft them ; that is to fay, if they ever had an idea of it. Nay, the author qf the *rights of man*, and the authorefs of the *rights of women*, are at this moment ftarving in a dirty dungeon, not a hundred paces from the *fanctum fanctorum* of liberty and equality ; and the poor unfortunate Goddefs* herfelf is guilliotined ! So much for liberty and the rights of man.

. The Tammany fociety comes forward in boafting of their " *venerable anceftors*," and, fays the Doctor in his anfwer: " Happy would *our* " venerable anceftors have been to have " found, &c." What ! Were they the Doctor's anceftors too ? I fuppofe he means in a figurative fenfe. But certainly, gentlemen, you made a *faux pas* in talking about your anceftors at all. It is always a tender fubject, and ought to be particularly avoided by a body of men " who difdain the fhackles of tradition."

You fay that, in the United States, " there " exifts a fentiment of free and candid enquiry, " which difdains the fhackles of tradition, pre- " paring a rich harveft of improvement and the " glorious triumph of truth." Knowing the religious, or rather irreligious, principles of the perfon to whom this fentence was addreffed, it is eafy to divine its meaning. But, without

---

* Madame Hebert, who had the honor of reprefenting this Deity, and who received for a confiderable time, the adorations and incenfe of the devout Parifians, was guilliotined not long ago. It is impoffible to fay for what fhe was executed, as the court by which fhe was tried do not wafte their precious time in committing their proceedings to writing.

F

to fay, *Idolatrous Chriftians*." Idolatrous Chriftians! It is the firft time I believe thefe two words were ever joined together. Is this the language of a man who wanted only toleration, in a country where the eftablifhed church, and the moft part of the diffenters alfo, are profeffedly *trinitarians?* He will undoubtedly fay that the people of this country are *idolators* too, for there is not one out of a hundred at moft, who does not firmly believe in the doctrine of the Trinity.

Such a man complains of perfecution with a very ill grace. But fuppofe he had been perfecuted for a mere matter of opinion ; it would be only receiving the meafure he has meted to others. Has he not approved of the unmerciful perfecution of the unfortunate and worthy part of the French clergy ; men as far furpaffing him in piety and utility as in fuffering ? They did not want to coin a new religion ; they wanted only to be permitted to enjoy, without interruption, the one they had been educated in, and that they had fworn in the moft folemn manner, to continue in to the end of their lives. The Doctor fays in his addrefs to the Methodifts ; " you will judge wether I have not reafon and " fcripture on my fide. You will at leaft be con- " vinced that *I have fo perfuaded myfelf* ; and you " cannot but refpect a real lover of truth, and " *a defire to bring others into it,* even in the man " who is unfortunately in an error." Does not this man blufh at approving of the bafe, cowardly and bloody perfecutions that have been carried on againft a fet of men, who erred, if they did err at all, from an excefs of con-

French themfelves have banifhed the very idea of the thing from amongft them ; that is to fay, if they ever had an idea of it. Nay, the author of the *rights of man*, and the authoref of the *rights of women*, are at this moment ftarving in a dirty dungeon, not a hundred paces from the *fanctum fanctorum* of liberty and equality ; and the poor unfortunate Goddef* herfelf is guilliotined ! So much for liberty and the rights of man.

The Tammany fociety comes forward in boafting of their " *venerable anceftors*," and, fays the Doctor in his anfwer: " Happy would *our* " venerable anceftors have been to have " found, &c." What ! Were they the Doctor's anceftors too ? I fuppofe he means in a figurative fenfe. But certainly, gentlemen, you made a *faux pas* in talking about your anceftors at all. It is always a tender fubject, and ought to be particularly avoided by a body of men " who difdain the fhackles of tradition."

You fay that, in the United States, " there " exifts a fentiment of free and candid enquiry, " which difdains the fhackles of tradition, pre- " paring a rich harveft of improvement and the " glorious triumph of truth." Knowing the religious, or rather irreligious, principles of the perfon to whom this fentence was addreffed, it is eafy to divine its meaning. But, without

* Madame Hebert, who had the honor of reprefenting this Deity, and who received for a confiderable time, the adorations and incenfe of the devout Parifians, was guilliotined not long ago. It is impoffible to fay for what fhe was executed, as the court by which fhe was tried do not wafte their precious time in committing their proceedings to writing.

F

to fay, *Idolatrous Chriſtians.*" Idolatrous Chriſtians! It is the firſt time I believe theſe two
words were ever joined together. Is this the
language of a man who wanted only toleration, in
a country where the eſtabliſhed church, and the
moſt part of the diſſenters alſo, are profeſſedly
trinitarians? He will undoubtedly fay that the
people of this country are *idolators* too, for
there is not one out of a hundred at moſt, who
does not firmly believe in the doctrine of the
Trinity.

Such a man complains of perſecution with a
very ill grace. But ſuppoſe he had been perſecuted for a mere matter of opinion; it would
be only receiving the meaſure he has meted to
others. Has he not approved of the unmerciful
perſecution of the unfortunate and worthy part
of the French clergy; men as far ſurpaſſing him
in piety and utility as in ſuffering? They did
not want to coin a new religion; they wanted
only to be permitted to enjoy, without interruption, the one they had been educated in, and
that they had ſworn in the moſt ſolemn manner,
to continue in to the end of their lives. The
Doctor fays in his addreſs to the Methodiſts;
" you will judge whether I have not reaſon and
" ſcripture on my ſide. You will at leaſt be con-
" vinced that *I have ſo perſuaded myſelf*; and you
" cannot but reſpect a real lover of truth, and
" *a deſire to bring others into it*, even in the man
" who is unfortunately in an error." Does
not this man bluſh at approving of the baſe,
cowardly and bloody perſecutions that have
been carried on againſt a ſet of men, who erred,
if they did err at all, from an exceſs of con-

ſcientiouſneſs? *He* talks of perſecution, and
puts on the mockery of woe: theirs has been
perſecution indeed. Robbed, dragged from
their homes, or obliged to hide from the ſight
of man, in continual expectation of the aſſaſſin's
ſtab; ſome tranſported, like common felons,
for ever; and a much greater number butchered by thoſe to whoſe happineſs their lives had
been devoted, and in that country that they loved
too well to diſgrace by their apoſtacy! How
gladly would one of thoſe unfortunate conſcien-
tious men have eſcaped to America, leaving fortune, friends and all behind him! And how
different has been the fate of Doctor Prieſtley!
Ah, Gentlemen! do not let us be deceived by
falſe pretenders: the manner of his emigration
is, of itſelf, a ſufficient proof that the ſtep was
not neceſſary, to the enjoyment of " protection
from violence."

You ſay, he has " long *diſintereſtedly* labour-
" ed for his country." 'Tis true he ſays ſo;
but we muſt not believe him more diſintereſted
than other reformers. If toleration had been all
he wanted; if he had contented himſelf with the
permiſſion of ſpreading his doctrines, he would
have found this in England, or in almoſt any
other country, as well as here. The man that
wants only to avoid perſecution, does not make
a noiſy and faſtidious diſplay of his principles, or
attack with unbridled indecency, the religion of
the country in which he lives. He who avoids perſecution is ſeldom perſecuted.

" The lifted ax, the agonizing wheel,
" Luke's iron crown and Damien's bed of ſteel.

every attempt to debafe chriftianity, in whatever fhape, and under whatever difguife it may appear.

In the addrefs of "the republican natives of "Great Britain and Ireland, refident at New "York," we find a very extraordinary paffage indeed. But, before we fay any thing about this addrefs, it will not be amifs to fay a word or two about the addreffers. I believe one might venture to fay, that there are but very few natives of Ireland among them; becaufe, the emigrants from that country, being generally engaged in agricultural purfuits from their firft arrival here, have not the time to form themfelves into political focieties: and the words "Great Britain" might probably have been fupplied by *one word*. However, as the gentlemen have not thought this word worthy of a place in their addrefs, I can by no means think of introducing it here. But let us fee what they fay of themfelves: " After a *fruitlefs oppofition* to a corrupt and " tyrannical government, *many of us, like you,* " fought freedom and protection in the United " States of America. We look back on our " native country with *pity* and *indignation*, at " the outrages that humanity has fuftained in " the perfons of the virtuous *Muir* and his pa- " triotic affociates." We may then fairly fuppofe, that thefe " republican natives of Great " Britain and Ireland" can be no other than the members of that renowned convention of which the " *virtuous* Muir," who is now fortunately on his paffage to Botany Bay, was prefident.

The paffage of their addrefs, alluded to above, is as follows; " Participating in the many blef-

" fings, which the government is calculated to
" infure, we are happy in giving it this proof of
" our refpectful attachment. We are only *griev-*
" *ed,* that a fyftem of fuch beauty and excellence
" fhould be at all *tarnifhed* by the exiftence of
" *flavery in any form;* but, as friends to the
" equal rights of man, we muft be permitted
" to fay, that we wifh thefe rights extended to
" every human being, *be his complexion what it*
" *may.* We however look forward with pleaf-
" ing anticipation to *a yet more perfect ftate of*
" *fociety;* and from that love of liberty which
" forms fo diftinguifhed a trait in the American
" character, are taught to hope that this *laft,*
" *this worft difgrace to a free government,* will
" finally and for ever be done away. " So !
Thefe gentlemen are hardly landed in the United
States before they begin to cavil againft the
government, and to pant after a *more perfect*
ftate of Society ! If they have already difcovered
that the fyftem is *tarnifhed* by *the very laft and*
worft difgrace of a free government, what may we
not reafonably expect from their future re-
fearches ? If they, with their virtuous Prefident,
had been landed in the fouthern ftates, they
might have lent a hand to finifh the great
work, fo happily begun by citizens Santhonax
and Polverel. They have caught the *itch* of
addreffing, petitioning and remonftrating in
their own country ; let them feratch themfelves
into a cure ; but let them not attempt fpread-
ing their diforder. They ought to remember,
that they are come here " to feek freedom and
" protection " *for themfelves,* and not *for others.*
When the people of thefe ftates are ready for a

G

total abolition of negro flavery, they will make a fhift to fee the propriety of adopting the mea-fure without the affiftance of thefe nothern lights. In the mean time, as the convention cannot here enter on their legiflative functions, they may amufe themfelves with a fable written for their particular ufe.

The Pot-Shop, a Fable.

In a pot-fhop well ftocked with ware of all forts, a difcontented ill formed pitcher un-luckily bore the fway. One day after the mor-tifying neglect of feveral cuftomers, " gentle-men," faid he, addreffing himfelf to his brown brethren in general, " gentlemen, with your " permiffion, we are a fet of tame fools, without " ambition, without courage : condemned to " the vileft ufes, we fuffer all without murmur-" ing. Let us dare to declare ourfelves, and " we fhall foon fee the difference. That fuperb " ewer, which, like us, is but earth ; thofe " gilded jars, vafes, china, and in fhort all " thofe elegant nonfenfes, whofe colours and " beauty have neither weight nor folidity, muft " yield to our ftrength and give place to our " fuperior merit. "

This civic harangue was received with peals of applaufe, and the pitcher (chofen prefident) became the organ of the affembly. Some, however, more moderate than the reft, attemp-ted to calm the minds of the multitude. But all thofe which are called jordans or chamber pots, were become intractable. Eager to vie with the bowls and cups, they were impatient almoſt to madneſs to quit their obſcure abodes, to ſhine upon the table, kiſs the lip and ornament the cup-board.

In vain did a wiſe water jug (ſome ſay it was a platter) make them a long and ſerious diſcourſe upon the peacefulneſs of their voca- " tion. Thoſe, " ſays he, " who are deſtined to " great employments are rarely the moſt happy. " We are all of the ſame clay, tis true ; but he " who made us, formed us for different func- " tions. One is for ornament, another for uſe. " The poſts the leaſt important are often the " moſt neceſſary. Our employments are ex- " tremely different, and ſo are our talents. "

This had a wonderful effect ; the moſt ſtupid began to open their ears : perhaps it would have ſucceded, if a greaſe pot had not cried out with a deciſive tone : " You reaſon like an aſs ; " to the devil with you and your ſilly leſ- " ſons."

Now the ſcale was turned again : all the hord of jordans, pans and pitchers applauded the ſuperior eloquence and reaſoning of the greaſe pot. In ſhort, they determined on the enter- prize ; but a diſpute aroſe who ſhould be chief : all would command and none obey. It was then you might have heard a clutter : pots, pans and pitchers, mugs, jugs and jordans, all put themſelves in motion at once ; and ſo wiſely and with ſo much vigour were their operations conducted that the whole was ſoon changed— not into china, but rubbiſh.

Let us leave the application of this fable to thoſe for whom it is intended, and come to the addreſs of " the aſſociated teachers in the city " of New-York. "

From the profeſſion of theſe gentlemen, one would have wiſhed not to find them among the Doctor's addreſſers ; and it will be for thoſe who employ the " aſſociated teachers " to judge, how far their approbation and praiſe of the writings of ſuch a man, is a proof of their being calculated for " the arduous and *important* " taſk of cultivating the human mind. " *
They very civilly invite the doctor to aſſiſt them to " *form the man* ; " and, in his anſwer, he ſeems to hint that he. may poſſibly accept the invitation. All I can ſay on this matter, is, if he ſhould embrace this profeſſion, I hope he will be exactly as ſuccefsful in forming the man, as he has been in reforming him.

In the anſwer to the " aſſociated Teachers, " the Doctor obſerves, that, *claſſes* of men, as well " as *individuals,* are apt to form *too high* ideas of " their *own importance.*" Never was a juſter obſervation than this, and never was this ob-ſervation more fully verified than in the parties themſelves. The Doctor's ſelf importance is ſufficiently depicted in the quotation that I have given from his letter to the people of Birming-ham ; and as for the " aſſociated teachers, " how familiarly ſoever they may talk of " the

---

* I have been informed, that theſe *aſſociated* brethren of the birch complain of my attacking them in the dark ; but let them lay their hands to their hearts, and ſay, if they can, that I fight more unfair than they do, when they diſ-charge their ill-humour on a poor little trembling wretch, whoſe pitiful look would ſoften the heart of a tiger. How-ever, I ceaſe the inglorious combat : I confeſs it is not fair to attack them with a pen. They know how to write with a rod only ; and I dare ſay their anſwer to my obſerva-tions on their addreſs is ſtill legible on the back-ſides of their unfortunate pupils.

" intriguing politics and vitiating refinements
" of the European World, " I mult fay, I
think, they know but little of what paffes in
that world ; or they never would have larded
with fuch extravagant eulogiums, productions,
which, in general, have been long exploded.

With refpect to the Doctor's metaphyfieal
reveries, or, in other words, his fyftem of infidelity, I fhall leave to himfelf the tafk of expo-
fing that to the deteftation of Americans, as it
has long been to that of the Englifh. * Of his
fcientific productions, I propofe, in a little time,
to give the public a fhort reveiw; † meanwhile I
refer the curious, reader to the publications of the
royal fociety, of 1791 and 1792, and to Doctor
Bewley's treatife on air. He will there fee his
fyftem of chemiftry and natural philofophy de-
tected, expofed and defeated ; and the " cele-
" brated philofopher " himfelf accufed and
convicted of plagiarifm. § He will there find
the key to the following fentence : " The
" *patronage* to be met with, in monarchical go-
" vernments, is ever *capricious*, and as often
" employed to bear down merit as to promote
" it, having for its object, not fcience, or any
" thing ufeful to mankind, but the mere repu-
" tation of the patron, *who is feldom any judge
" of fcience.* " ‡ This is the language of every
foured neglected author, from a forry ballad

* He has made a pretty good beginning already, as we
fhall fee by and by.
† The Doctor has faved me the trouble of doing this.
§ Have a little patience, reader, and you fhall be fatis-
fied of this.
‡ This was addreffed to the Philofophical fociety at
Philadelphia. We fhall fee all this unravelled by and by.

monger to a doctor with half a dozen initials at the end of his name.

As to his talents as a writer we have only to open our eyes to be convinced that they are far below mediocrity. His ftyle is uncouth and fuperlatively diffufe. Always involved in *minutiæ,* every fentence is a ftring of parenthefifes, in finding the end of which, the reader is lucky if he does not lofe the propofition they were meant to illuftrate. In fhort, the whole of his phrafeology is extremely difgufting; to which may be added, that even in point of grammar he is very often incorrect.

As a proof of what I have here afferted, I could give a thoufand fentences from his writings; but I choofe one or two from his anfwers to the addreffers, as thefe pieces are in every body's hands; and, not to criticife unfairly, I fhall take the firft fentence I come at. It runs thus:

 " Viewing with the deepeft concern, as you " do, the profpect that is now exhibited in " Europe, thofe troubles which are the natural " offspring of their forms of government, ori- " ginating indeed in the fpirit of liberty, but " gradually degenerating into tyrannies, equal- " ly degrading to the rulers and the ruled, I " rejoice in finding an affylum from perfecu- " tion in a country in which thofe abufes have " come to a natural termination, and produced " another fyftem of liberty, founded on fuch " wife principles, as I truft, will guard againft " all future abufes; thofe artificial diftinctions " in fociety, from which they fprung, being " completely eradicated, that protection from

" violence, which laws and government promise
" in all countries, but which I have not found
" in my own, I doubt not I shall find with you,
" though I cannot promise to be a better subject
" of this government, than my whole conduct
" will evince that I have been to that of Great
" Britain."

This is neither the *style periodique*, nor the *style coupé*, it is I presume the *style entortillé* : for one would certainly think that the author had racked his imagination to render what he had to say unintelligible. This sentence of monstrous length is cut asunder in the middle by a semicolon, which, except that it serves the weary reader by way of half way house, might be placed in any other part of the sentence to, at least, equal advantage. In fact, this is not a sentence ; it is a rigmarole ramble, that has neither beginning nor ending, and conveys to us no idea of any thing but the author's incapacity.

" Viewing with the deepest concern as you
" do, the prospect that is now exhibited in Eu-
" rope, those *troubles* which are the natural off-
" spring of THEIR forms of government." What, in the name of goodness, does this mean ?— *Troubles* is the only antecedent that can be found to *their*, and the necessary conclusion is, *troubles have their forms of government.*

The doctor says, in his answer to the Tammany society : " Happy would our venerable
" ancestors, as you justly call them, *have been*,
" to *have found* America such a retreat to
" them." It may perhaps be useful to the learned Doctor to know, that he ought to have

faid " Happily would our venerable anceftors,
" as you juftly call them, have been, *to find*
" America, &c."

I grant that there is great reafon to believe,
that the Doctor was refolved to be as dull as his
addreffers ; but I affert that it is impoffible for a
perfon accuftomed to commit his thoughts to
paper with the fmalleft degree of tafte or cor-
rectnefs, to fall into fuch grofs folecifms, or to
tack phrafes together in fuch an awkward home,
fpun manner. In fhort, he cannot be fit for
even the poft of *caftigator* ; and therefore it is
to be hoped that the " affociated teachers" will
not leffen their " importance" by admitting
him amongft them ; that is to fay, except it be
as a pupil.

There are many things that aftonifh us in the
addreffes, amongft which the *compaffion* that the
addreffers exprefs for that " *infatuated*" and
" *devoted country*," Great Britain, certainly is
not the leaft.

The Democratic fociety, with a hatred againft
tyranny, that would have become the worthy
nephew of Damien,*or the great Marat himfelf,
fay : " The multiplied oppreffions which cha-
" racterife that government, excite in us, the
" moft painful fenfations and exhibit a fpecta-
" cle as difgufting in itfelf as difhonorable to
" the Britifh name."

And what a tender affectionate concern do
the fons of Tammany exprefs for the poor diftreffed unfortunate country of their " venerable
" anceftors." " A country," fay they, " al-

* Robefpierre.

" though now prefenting a profpect frightful to
" the eye of humanity, yet *once* the nurfe of
" fciences, of arts, of heroes, and of freemen, a
" country which although at prefent apparent-
" ly *devoted to deftruction*, we *fondly* hope may
" yet *tread back the fteps of infamy and ruin*, and
" *once more rife confpicuous among the free nations*
" of the earth."

But of all the addreffers none feem fo zealous
on this fubject as " the republican natives of
Great Britain and Ireland. " " While, " fay
they, " we look back on our native country
" with emotions of pity and indignation, at the
" outrages human nature has fuftained, in the
" perfons of the virtuous *Muir* and his patrio-
" tic affociates ; and deeply lament the fatal
" apathy into which our *countrymen* have fallen :
" we defire to be thankful to the great author.
" of our being, that we are in America and
" that it has pleafed him, in his wife provi-
" dence, to make thefe United States an Afy-
" lum, not only from the immediate tyranny of
" the Britifh government, but alfo from thofe
" impending calamities, which its increafing
" defpotifm, and multiplied iniquities, muft
" infallibly bring down on a deluded and op-
" preffed people. " What an enthufiaftic
warmth is here ! No folemn-league-and-cove-
nant prayer, embellifhed with the nafal fweet-
nefs of the conventicle, was ever more affect-
ing.

To all this the Doctor very pitioufly echoes
back " figh for figh, and groan for groan ; and
" when the fountain of their eyes is dry, his
" fupplies the place and weeps for both. "

H

There is fomething fo pathetic, fo irrefiftably moving in all this, that a man muft have a hard heart indeed to read it, and not burft into laughter.

In fpeaking of Monarchies, it has often been lamented that the fovereign feldom, or never hears the truth; and much afraid I am, that this is equally applicable to democracies. What court fycophants are to a prince, demagogues are to a people; and the latter kind of parafites is by no means lefs dangerous than the former; perhaps more fo, as being more ambitious and more numerous. God knows, there were too many of this defcription in America, before the arrival of Doctor Prieftley: I can therefore fee no reafon for boaftings and addreffings on account of the acquifition.

Every one muft obferve, how the doctor has fallen at once into the track of thofe, who were already in poffeffion of the honourable poft. Finding a popular prejudice prevailing againft his country, and not poffeffing that *patriæ caritas*, which is the characteriftic of his countrymen, he has not been afhamed to attempt making his court by flattering that prejudice. I grant that a prejudice againft this nation is not only excufable, but almoft commendable in *Americans*; but the misfortune is, it expofes them to deception, and makes them the fport of every intriguing adventurer. Suppofe it be the intereft of Americans that Great Britain fhould be ruined and, even annihilated, in the prefent conteft; it can never be their intereft to believe that this defirable object is already nearly or quite accomplifhed, at a time when fhe is become more formidable than ever, in every quarter of

the globe. And with refpect to the internal
fituation of that country, we ought not to fuffer ourfelves to be deceived by " gleanings
" from morning chronicles, or Dublin ga-
" zettes :" for, if we infift that newfpaper report is the criterion by which we ought to judge
of the governments, and the ftate of other countries, we muft allow the fame meafure to foreigners with refpect to our own country ; and then
what muft the people of England think of the
government of the United States, upon reading
a page or two from the flovenly pen of *Agricola.*

" It is charitable," fays this democrat, " It
" is charitable to believe many who figned the
" conftitution, never dreamed of the meafures
" taking place, which alas! we now experience.
" By this double government, we are involved
" in unneceffary burdens which *neither we nor*
" *our fathers* ever knew. Such a *monfter of a*
" *government* has feldom ever been known on
" earth. We are obliged to maintain two go-
" vernments, with their full number of officers
" from head to foot. Some of them receive
" fuch wages as never were heard of before in
" any goverment upon earth ; and all this be-
" ftowed on *Ariftocrats* for doing next to noth-
" ing. A bleffed revolution! a bleffed revolu-
" tion indeed! but farmers, mechanics and
" labourers have no fhare in it, we are the affes
" who muft have the honor of paying them
" all without any adequate fervice. Now let
" the impartial judge whether our government
" taken collectively, anfwers the great end of
" *protecting our perfons and property!* Or whether
" it is not rather calculated to drain us of our
" money, and give it to men who have not

" rendered adequate fervice for it. Had an
" infpired prophet told us the things which
" our eyes fee,. in the beginning of the revolu-
" tion, he might have met Jeremiah's fate ; or
" if we had believed him, *not one in a thoufand*
" *would have refifted Great Britain.* Indeed, my
" countrymen, we are fo loaded by our new
" governments, that we can have little heart to
" attempt to move under all our burdens ; we
" have this confolation, when things come to
" the worft, there muft be a change, and *we*
" *may reft fatisfied, that either the federal or ftate*
" *governments muft fall.*"

If " gleanings" like thefe were publifhed in
England, would not the people naturally ex-
claim : What ! the boafted government of A-
merica come to this already ? The poor Americans are dreadfully tyrannized by the Ariftocrats ! There will certainly be a *revolution* in
America foon ! They would be juft as much
miftaken as the people in this country are, when
they talk of a revolution in England.

Neither ought we to look upon the emigration of perfons from England to this country as
a proof of their being perfecuted, and of the
tyranny of the Englih government. It is paying
America a very poor compliment, to fuppofe
that nothing fhort of perfecution, could bring
fettlers to 's fhores. This is befides the moft
unfortunate proof that could poffibly be produced by the advocates of the French Revolution :
for if the emigration of a perfon to this country
be a proof of a tyranny cxifting in that from
which he comes, how fuperlatively tyrannical
muft the government in France be ? But they
fay, thofe who emigrate from France are Arif-

tocrats : they are not perfecuted; they emigrate becaufe they *hate a free country.* What!
do they really come to *America* becaufe they *hate
a free country?* Did the governors of Martinico,
&c. make a capitulation to be fent here, *to avoid
going to a free country?* The Democratic fociety
will certainly oblige the world very much in
explaining this enigma.

I am one of thofe, who wifh to believe that
foreigners come to this country from choice,
and not from neceffity. America opens a wide
field for entreprize; wages for all mechanics are
better, and the means of fubfiftence proportio-
nably cheaper than in Europe. This is what
brings foreigners amongft us : they become
citizens of America for the honeft purpofes of
commerce, of turning their induftry and talents
to the beft account, and of bettering their for-
tunes. By their exertions to enrich themfelves,
they enrich the ftate, lower the wages, and render
the country lefs dependent upon others. The
moft numerous as well as the moft ufeful are
mechanics ; perhaps a cobler with his hammer
and awls, is a more valuable acquifition than a
dozen philofophi-theologi-politi-cal empiricks
with all their boafted apparatus.

Of all the Englifh arrived in thefe States
(fince the war) no one was ever calculated to
render them lefs fervice than Doctor Prieftley;
and what is more, perhaps no one (before or
fince, or even in the war) ever intended to
render them lefs : his preference to the American government is all affectation : his emigration was not voluntary : he ftaid in England
till he faw no hopes of recovering a loft reputation ; and then, burfting with envy and refent-

ment, he fled into what the Tammany society very justly call " banishment," covered with the universal detestation of his countrymen.

Here ended the pamphlet in its original form, concluding with some of those assertions which were said to be the most " hazarded," and for the truth of which I am sorry I have no better voucher than the Doctor himself.

In the preface to his farewell sermon, preached to his disciples at Hackney, he says : " I hope " my friends, and the public, will indulge me " while I give the reasons of its being the last, " in consequence of my having at length, after " much hesitation, and *now with reluctance*, come " to a resolution to leave the kingdom. "—— " I cannot refrain from repeating that I leave " my country with *real regret.* "

Was it a " hazarded assertion " then, to say that his preference to the American government was all affectation, and that his emigration was not voluntary ?

" My friends, " says he, " earnestly advised " me to disguise myself as I was going to London. " But all that was done in that way was taking " a place for me in the mail coach, which I " entered at Worcester, in another name than " my own. However, the friend who had the " courage to receive me in London, had thought " it necessary to provide a dress that should " disguise me, and also a method of making my " escape, in case the house should have been at- " tacked on my account; and for some time my " friends would not suffer me to appear in the " streets. "—— " The managers of one of the

" principal charities among the diffenters ap-
" plied to me to preach their annual fermon,
" and I confented. But the treafurer, a man
" of fortune, was fo alarmed at it, that he de-
" clared he could not fleep. I therefore, to his
" great relief, declined preaching at all. " ——
" When the Hackney affociation was formed,
" feveral fervants in the neighbourhood ac-
" tually removed their goods ; and when there
" was fome political meeting at the houfe of
" Mr. Breillat, though about two miles from
" my houfe, a woman whofe daughter was fer-
" vant in the houfe contiguous to mine, came
" to her miftrefs, to entreat that fhe might be
" out of the way. " — " On feveral occafions
" the neighbourhood has been greatly alarmed
" on account of my being fo near them. I
" could name a perfon, and to appearance a
" reputable tradefman, who declared that, in
" cafe of any difturbance they would immedi-
" ately come to Hackney, evidently for the
" purpofe of mifchief. In this ftate of things,
" it is not to be wondered at, that, of many fer-
" vants who were recommended to me, and
" fome that were actually hired, very few could,
" for a long time, be prevailed upon to live with
" me. " * — " My eldeft fon was fettled in a
" bufinefs, which promifed to be very advan-
" tageous, at Manchefter ; but his partner,
" though a man of liberality himfelf, informed
" him, on perceiving the general prevalence of
" the fpirit which produced the riots in Bir-
" mingham, that, owing to his relationfhip to

* Servants in *England* have a character to preferve, I
fuppofe

" *me*, he was under the neceffity of propofing a
" feparation, which accordingly took place. "
— " Many times, I have been burnt in effigy
" along with Mr. Paine ; and numberlefs in-
" fulting and threatening letters have been fent
" to me from *all parts of the kingdom* " —
" Ill treated as I had been, not merely by the
" populace of Birmingham, but by *the country*
" *in general*, and afterwards by the *Reprefenta-*
" *tives of the Nation* , * I own I was not without
" deliberating on the fubject of emigration. "

Was it a " hazarded affertion" then, to fay
that he fled into banifhment, covered with the
univerfal deteftation of his countrymen ?

But, though the above quotations moft am-
ply prove that he was detefted by the whole
nation, from the Peer to the Parifh-Boy, and
that he was a volunteer emigrant, about as
much as one of the hurlers that oar tarpawlings
catch on the coaft of Ireland, yet the real caufe
of his emigration remains to be explained.

While the Birmingham affair was frefh in the
Doctor's mind, he fays that he had fome thoughts
of emigration ; but that all things confidered,
he " determined to ftay in England, expofed as
" he was to every kind of obloquy and infult."
He therefore went to Hackney, to fucceed his
dear-friend and fellow labourer of factious memory, Doctor Price. Here, as appears by his
own words above quoted, the people diflike

---

* He might have made an exception or two here ; for,
among the lords, he had for advocate the Earl of Stanhope,
whom an Englifh author very aptly compares to *Praife-*
God Bare-Bones ; and, among the commons, he had the
immaculate Charles Fox. A fingle word of praife from
men like thefe would blaft the character of a Saint.

him fo much, that he was obliged to remove to Clapton. At this place he found the peace and tranquillity he fought, and for that reafon, fays he, " I took a long leafe of my houfe, and expend-
" ed a confiderable fum in improving it. I alfo
" determined, with the affiftance of my friends,
" to refume my philofophical and other purfuits;
" and after an interruption amounting to about
" two years, it was with a pleafure that
" I cannot defcribe, that I entered my new la-
" boratory, and began the moft common pre-
" paratory proceffes, with a view to fome *origi-*
" *nal enquiries.*"

Here then we fee him (in the month of Auguft, 1793) in quiet poffeffion of every thing he wanted to enjoy. What then could make him come off to America fo foon after? If he had determined to ftay, when expofed to every kind of obloquy and infult, what could make him fly away when no longer expofed to it? It muft be allowed that the Doctor's paffion for controverfy and perfecution is fuch as would excufe a belief that he grew angry with the people for letting him alone; but candour obliges me to confefs that this was not the cafe in the prefent inftance; for, he was going on very diligently with his proceffes and his " original enquiries." Yes, reader, it was thefe curfed " *original* enquiries" that did all the mifchief. For, the Doctor being in the height of them, happened to fall upon a WONDERFUL DISCOVERY, which, though *erroneous* was not *original.* However, all would yet have been fafe, if he had kept it within the walls of his laboratory; but his communicative temper would not permit him to do this, and the unfortu-

I

nate *wonderful difcovery* made its public entry
into the book-feller's fhops on the 16th of November, 1793.

This brought him a " *New Year's Gift*" from
Doctor Harrington, his old antagonift and his
conqueror, as we fhall fee by the following extract from the gentleman's Magazine for May,
1794.

" Doctor Prieftley, immediately after the
" Birmingham riots might be fuppofed to have
" real caufe of alarm.   But as his refolution
" withftood the firft fury of the flood, it
" is rather extraordinary that he fhould now
" all at once turn coward, and fly to America.
" He muft furely be greatly at a lofs for folid
" reafons, when he thinks it worth while to ad-
" vance fuch trifling circumftances as the gof-
" fiping of his fervant-maid with the neighbours,
" or the foolifh declaration of an individual
" before one of his congregation.   But, that
" the Doctor was able to brave thefe dreadful
" denunciations and the terrors of his maid,
" appears from his venturing to take a long
" leafe of his houfe, expending a confiderable
" fum of money upon it, and accepting the
" contributions of his friends towards another
" apparatus, laboratory, &c.   The Doctor, as
" a prudent man, would certainly not have ex-
" pended his money thus, had he not fully de-
" termined again to remain in the kingdom."

" Then what, give me leave to afk, Mr.
" Urban, can have fo lately happened to make
" him alter his refolution ?   As there appears to
" be fomething which the Doctor is at pains

" to conceal, it may be worth while to enquire
" what it is."

" Doctor Prieftly, Sir, for many years, had
" been acquiring a very high degree of fame
" from his chemical and philofophical experi-
" ments. According to his own account, it
" was this great reputation which gave him fo
" much confequence in the eyes of the French
" philofophers, and which fanctioned his other
" purfuits. On the 16th of November laft, he
" pubiifhed a pamphlet in a very boafting and
" exulting ftyle, informing the world, that he
" had made a moft important difcovery, that
" water was formed of dephlogifticated and
" phlogifticated airs ; the fame airs, and the
" fame proportions, which your correfpondent
" Doctor Harrington obferves, that the Hon-
" ourable Mr. Cavendifh, from his miftaken ex-
" periments, confiders as conftituting the ni-
" trous acid. The abfurdity of thefe opinions
" has been pointed out by Doctor Harrington
" in your Magazine for January and February
" laft ; in which it is moft clearly and fatisfacto-
" rily fhown in what manner Doctor Prieftley
" was miftaken : proving at the fame time the
" real formation of the different airs, difplaying
" the very great futility and the errors of our
" modern chemiftry ; and at the fame time,
" bringing the very heavy charge of plagiarifm
" upon Doctor Prieftley." *

" As Doctor Prieftley, in this laft pamphlet,
" announced his intentions of publifhing again
" very foon, having materials for another by

* See the *New Year's Gift,* to Dr. Prieftley. Gentlemen's
Magazine, for Jan. and Feb. 1794.

" him, expressing apprehensions lest any per-
" son should interfere with him in these experi-
" ments, I expected every day to hear of the
" Doctor's vindicating himself and his opinions,
" answering the charges of Doctor Harrington,
" or acknowledging his philosophical mistakes.
" Instead of which, to my very great surprize,
" I am informed he is stealing off to America ;
" thus leaving his antagonist master of the
" field, and only saying that the world may hear
" of him again in his chemical pursuits. This
" is certainly very different from what he gave
" us reason to expect, when he announced to
" the world, in his ostentatious pamphlet, that
" we might expect to hear regularly from him.
" But I think, you will agree with me, that
" he has totally fled from his aërial chemistry,
" and, what is the most awkward and extraor-
" dinary thing of all, without one word of de-
" fence from the charges of philosophical pla-
" giarism."
" It was not till Doctor Priestley received the
" New Year's Gift of your January and Fe-
" bruary Magazine, that he was in earnest a-
" about America. And, I am informed, that
" he was so much afraid that he should receive
" another from the same valuable work, that he
" got on board the ship the very evening before
" the Magazine for the month of March made
" its appearance, although the ship was not like-
" ly to sail immediately."

Was it a " hazarded assertion " then, to say
that the great philosopher was accused and convicted of plagiarism, and that he staid in England till he saw no hopes of recovering a lost
reputation ?

It has been already obferved, that the Doctor
merited the univerfal odium he laboured under
in England, and we find nothing in his juftifi-
catory preface to his farewell fermon (which
was re-publifhed at Philadelphia as an indirect
anfwer to the firft edition of this pamphlet) that
ought to induce us to reject this opinion. For.
it certainly will not be pretended that his being
hated by King, Lords and Commons, by high
and low, rich and poor, churchmen and diffenters, proves him to be an innocent inoffenfive
man : on the contrary, if that trivial and favourite republican maxim, " the voice of the
people is the voice of God," be founded in
truth, then does the Doctor ftand condemned
by God as well as man.

But let us hear a little of what he fays in his
vindication.

After ftating that he had been unjuftly charged with being a feditious, factious politician, he
fays ; " let any one only caft his eyes over the
" long lift of my publications, and he will fee
" that they relate almoft wholly to *theology*, &c."
And he has taken care to publifh this lift at
Philadelphia, amounting to *feventy five* different works. Yes, "by thy works fhalt thou
" be judged," but not by the *number* of them.

He tells us he hardly ever meddled with *politics*,
and in the very next paragraph, acknowledges that
he wrote a fmall anonymous pamphlet (when
he was a younger man) in favour of *Wilkes and
Liberty*. Mr. Wilkes has had the good fenfe to
retract moft of the wild notions that the Doctor
wrote to defend, and happy would it have been
for the latter if he had profited from age, and

from the example of his patron. Mr. Wilkes is now a determined champion of that constitution that the Doctor wanted to destroy, and accordingly, he occupies one of the first offices in the first city in the world, while Doctor Priestley is a very insignificant settler, in a town consisting of a couple of hundred of wooden houses.

Another work he wrote, addressed to the dissenters, on the subject of the approaching war with America ; which he says was *distributed in great numbers by his friends*, and *not without effect.* The subject of this work, and the good it was intended to do *his* country are easily conceived, as he tells us it was written at the *request* of *Doctor Franklin*—He does not tell us whether he was paid in sterling or continental money for this work.

On this occasion the reader will please to bear in mind, that I am not pretending that *we* ought to dislike Doctor Priestley ; for he is certainly as much entitled to our gratitude and esteem as Arnold was to that of the British.

After this he says he meddled no more with *politics ;* " except as far as the business of the " *Test Act*, and all *civil establishments of religion*, had a concern with politics."* And yet he was *no factious politician !*

* This is the great stumbling block of the English Dissenters. What can there be in this *Test Act*, that makes them so unhapppy ? Why, it prevents them from obtaining——not the *kingdom of heaven*, but *lucrative employments.* Is it not amazing, that people, who are so very godly that they cannot conform to the established religion of the country, should trouble themseleves about places and pensions ? They are continually telling us that their kingdom is not of

Boasting of his intimate connexion with Doctors Price and Franklin is a drole way of proving the peaceablenefs of his difpofition, and his attachment to his country. With full as much reafon might he boaft of being a relation of *Jenny Cameron* or *Guy Fawkes*.

Franklin, Price and Prieftley! A precious trio! well worthy of each other. Methinks I fee them now in one of their dark confultations, like the three Weird Sifters round their cauldron, brewing

    " Double, double, toil and trouble ;

    " Fire burn and cauldron bubble."

As for Benjamin Franklin, Efqr. and Soap Boiler, his character for *peaceablenefs* is as well known as his character for *gratitude* and *integrity*; and moft people knows that the " political divine," Price, fpent the greateft part of a too long life in endeavouring to blow up the flames of rebellion in England. He was one of the principal projectors of the famous college of diffenting Jefuits at Hackney; from whence were to come the Titus Oatefes of an Unitarian Plot. *

this world, and yet they want to reign. I think, however, it would be but right to grant them whatHelvetius was willing to grant the Priefts; every thing *above* the tops of the houfes.

    * When this pious old Apoftle of difcord heard of the triumphs of the Paris mob, and of the bloody fcenes that enfued, he exclaimed : " Lord now let thy fervant depart " in peace for mine eyes have feen thy *falvation* ". Pretty *falvation* truely. According to my ideas of *damnation*, the fcenes that have taken place in France fince the Revolution,

It is pretty clear that the preface, to which I have been fo often obliged, was intended more to procure the Doctor a favourable reception *here*, than to reconcile him to his countrymen ; and, in this refpect, the thing was prudent, though the publifhing of it in England was certainly a trait of infolence, unparalleled even in the annals of Unitarianifm. It was courting a kick on the breech by way of farewell falute; but even in this he was difappointed, and was as laft obliged to come off without or even fo much as a box on the ear, to afford an excufe for his whining, and for the milk-fop fighs of the New-York Societies.

I have heard many grave people, and by no means anarchifts, exprefs a forrow for the ill ufage Doctor Prieftley received in England. But *how* was he ill ufed ?—He was threatned ;—people would not let him into their houfes ; —fervants would not live with him ; — a farmer would not learn his fon hufbandry ; — a mechanic turned another fon out of his partnerfhip; —Doctor Horfly would not fubcribe to his antichriftian theology, nor Doctor Harrington to his aërial chemiftry. Well, and what then? Do we call this ill ufuage ? Grant me patience! have not the people of England a right to like and diflike whom they pleafe, as well as the people of America ?

If, as I have already obferved, he had fallen into the hands of a French mob — but ftop; we have no occafion to crofs the fea. If he had

refemble it as much as any think on earth can do. I am fure there has been a continual " weeping and wailing and gnafhing of teeth ".

fallen into the hands of an American mob, how would he have fared? Let us fee.

"About twelve perfons, armed and painted "black, in the night of the 10th of June, broke. "into the houfe of *John Lynn*, where the office "was kept, and after having feduced him to "come down ftairs, and put himfelf in their "power, they feized him, threatened to hang "him, took him to a retired fpot in the neigh- "bouring wood; and there, after cutting off. "his hair, tarring and feathering him, fwore "him never again to allow the ufe of his houfe "for an excife office: having done which, they "bound him naked to a tree, and left him in "that fituation till morning. Not content with "this, the malcontents, fome days after, made "him another vifit; pulled down part of his "houfe, and put him in a fituation to be obliged "to become an exile from his home, and to "find an *afylum* elfewhere."

This is no " hazarded affertion," at any rate; unlefs Mr. Hamilton hazarded it; for it is taken from his report to the Prefident of the United States.

This mob ftopped the mail, cut open the bag, and took out the letters. This mob *killed* feveral perfons, took others prifoner, and ufed the *Marfhall* in particular extremely cruelly: they even went fo far as to prefent their pieces at him with every appearance of an intention to affaffinate. And yet neither the *Marfhall* nor *Lynn* has ever had any thoughts of *emigrating*.

Has any thing of this kind ever happened to Doctor Prieftley? Has the weight of a fingle

K

finger, ever been laid upon him, or any of his family? "You have," say the addressers at New-York, "fled from the rude arm of vio-"lence, from the *rod* of lawless power:—We "have learned with regret and indignation the "abandoned proceedings of those spoilers who "destroyed your house and goods, ruined your "philosophical apparatus and library, commit-"ted to the flames your manuscripts, pryed into "the secrets of your private papers, and in their "*barbarian fury* put your life itself in *danger*.— "We enter, Sir, with emotion and sympathy "into the numerous sacrifices you must have "made, to an undertaking which so eminently "exhibits our country, as an asylum for the "persecuted and oppressed." All this was extremely apropos in the midst of the Western insurrection. If it was "*barbarian fury*" to put *life in danger*, what was it to *take life away?* The people over the mountains seem to have revolted on purpose to make these addressers a laughing stock. Are they not ashamed to have made a canting sympathetic address to a stranger, whose sufferings, if real, they knew nothing about, while they have borne with a more than stoic firmness, and *without a single address*, the well known sufferings of their own countrymen? They want the Pittsburg affair forgotten; why then do they want to perpetuate the memory of the Birmingham riots? "Thou hypocrite, first "cast the beam out of thine own eye; and then "shalt thou see clearly to cast the mote out "of thy brother's eye."

The Doctor complains again in his preface, of partiality in the courts of justice; and says,

" I am not unaffected by the unexampled pu-
" nifhments of Mr. *Muir* and my *friend* Mr.
" *Palmer*, for offences, which, if, in the eye of
" reafon, they be any at all, are flight, and *very*
" *infufficiently proved.* But the fentence of Mr.
" *Winterbotbom*, for delivering form the pulpit
" *what I am perfuaded he never did deliver*, and
" which, fimilar evidence might have drawn
" down on myfelf, has fome thing in it ftill
" more alarming." Aye, aye, very alarming,
without doubt, but nothing like Doctor Har-
rinton's New years gift.

This is another pretty bold trait of modefty
and moderation. Here are three courts of juftice, three grand and three petty juries all condemned in the lump. If what the Doctor fays
be true, then were the Englifh all become a neft
of fcoundrels and purgerers, except his innocent
felf, his three fons, and his worthy *friends* the
Botany-Bay Convicts; but, if what he fays be
not true, what did he deferve at the hands of
the Englifh, for thus aiming a ftab at their
reputation ?

There are fome among us, who pretend
to have a belief in this partial juftice in Great
Britain ; and the hobgoblin accounts of it have
been noifed about thefe ftates, in a ftyle that
would have founded well from the top of a
chimney or, at the bar of a brothel ; but,
unfortunately for our political vultures, the trial
of *Hardy* has undeceived every one that is capa-
ble of thinking.

When the account of this trial firft arrived,

it caufed nearly as great joy, among fome people, as did the " *taking* of *Amfterdam* " or the fending of " the *Duke of York* to Paris in an *iron cage* ;" in fact, it was almoft of feftivic confequence. But this was foon perceived to be an egregious blunder. People began to reflect. What, faid they, there is fome juftice left in England then? The nation is not become " one *infular Baftile* ?"

What a chance would poor *Hardy* have ftood before the Revolutionary Tribunal at Paris or Bordeaux? Would he have had *eight days* trial? Would he have had *eight minutes?* Would the *fans-culotte* populace have carried him home amidft acclamations? No ; unlefs it had been to his laft home. It appears that Meffrs. Erfkine and Gibbs have received great and deferved applaufe for their able defence of an innocent man, and that the government has not touched a hair of their heads. —Where is Monfieur *De Malfherbe*, the generous *De Malfherbe*, who ftepped forth at the age of 75 to defend his innocent and deferted Sovereign? —— Where is he?—Numbered with the dead! Gone to the receptacle of all that was eftimable in France! —— Neither his admired talents, his long and eminent fervices, his generous fidelity, his gray hairs, nor his fpotlefs life, could fave him from the fury of thofe regenerated ruffians whom Doctor Prieftley does not blufh to call his " dear fellow citizens. " *

Every man that is condemned in England, whether it be by the public voice or by a court of

---

* Monfr. De Seze, the fecond counfel of Louis XVI, faved his life by flight.

juſtice, is ſure, according to ſome people, to be vilely treated. — The people are ſlaves; — the jury was packed. —— But how would this meaſure ſuit if meted to ourſelves? A fellow, who was hanged here the other day, told the crowd, juſt as he was going off, that he had no doubt but the greateſt part of them merited the ſame fate. * This " farewell ſermon " was full as modeſt as Doctor Prieſtley's; but if the Engliſh were to pretend to believe that the majority of us deſerve the halter, ſhould we not call them a ſet of narrow-ſouled, ill-natured, envious wretches? Certainly we ſhould, and with a great deal of juſtice too.

I ſhould here put an end to my obſervations, flattering myſelf that the whole buſineſs of the Doctor's emigration has been ſet in a pretty fair light; but, as he has lately publiſhed ſomething, which he calls an *Anſwer* to Paine's *Age of Reaſon*, and, as he there attempts to wipe off the charge of *deiſm*, I look upon myſelf as called upon to ſay a word or two in reply.

This *Anſwer* conſiſts of a number of letters, addreſſed to the *philoſophers* in France, and to a *philoſophical* unbeliever. In the preface, the Doctor ſays: " The more I attend to this ſub- " ject, the more ſenſible I am that no defence " of chriſtianity can be of any avail 'till it be " freed from the many *corruptions* and abuſes " which have *hitherto* encumbered it." Among theſe *corruptions* he numbers, *atonement*, *incarna-tion* and the *trinity*; and, ſays he: " The *expo-* " *ſing* of theſe *corruptions* I therefore think to be

---

* See the American Daily Advertiſer.

" the moft eſſential preliminary to the defence
" of chriſtianity, and confequently I ſhall omit
" no fair opportunity of reprobating them in
" the ſtrongeſt terms, to whatever odium I
" may expoſe myſelf." He has been as good
as his word ; for, the whole piece appears to be
an attack on the doctrine of the *trinity* rather
than an *Anſwer* to Paine. *

He begins the firſt letter with telling us, that
he has, " read with pleaſure, and even with en-
" thuſiaſm, the *admirable* report of Robeſpierre
" on the ſubject of morals and religion." Now,
it is well known, that this report contained a regular plan for eſtabliſhing a *deiſtical* worſhip in
France ; and it is alſo well known, that Paine
wrote his book to flatter Robeſpierre, and by that
means to procure his own diſcharge from priſon. How comes it then that the Doctor ſhould
admire the principles of the one, and pretend to
anſwer thoſe of the other ?

He very artfully cries off all acquaintance
with Voltaire, Rouſſeau and Gibbon ; but
he knows they are in a place whence they
cannot anſwer him. However, Gibbon left him
a letter that he ought not to have forgotten ſo

* If the reader looks over the firſt and ſecond chapters of
the Goſpel according to St. Matthew, he will ſee every
thing that is neceſſary to confirm him in the doctrines that
Doctor Prieſtley thinks it his duty to *reprobate in the ſtrongeſt terms.* But the Doctor gets rid of this proof, which he
knows to be in every one's hands, by telling us that thoſe
two chapters are " ſpurious ;" that is to ſay, *falſe.* This is
a knock-me-down argument. He will certainly tell us that
the firſt chapter of the Goſpel of St. John is " ſpurious"
alſo ; and thus he may go on, 'till he leaves us but juſt e-
nough text to make up an Unitarian Creed.

foon.——The Doctor, having no *wonderful difcovery* upon his hands, wrote to Mr. Gibbon,
not long before the death of the latter, challeng-
ing him to the combat. This Mr. Gibbon
very politely declined, by saying, that he could
never bring himself to difpute with a perfon
from whofe writings he had in a great meafure
imbibed his principles ; adding, that if the Doctor was really become a convert to chriftianity
fince he had received the laft anfwer from Doc- .
tor Horfley, he thought, the propable remainder
of his life was by no means too long to repair
the injury the former part of it had done ; and
therefore, advifed him not to lofe his time in
vain and unprofitable difpute. If the Doctor
had followed this falutary advice, we fhould
have been fpared the pain of feeing an old man
turned of fixty amufing, himfelf and the world
with a fham anfwer to the wild incoherent blaf-
phemy of a poor unhappy wretch, whom difa-
pointment and hunger had driven to defpair,
and who would have turned Turk, Jew, or even
Eunuch, for an extraordinary bifcuit or a
bundle of ftraw.*

The Doctor boafts of his having been elected
a Deputy to the National Convention, and
ftyles himfelf their " *highly honored* fellow citi-
" zen." It is fubject both of wonder and regret, that he did not prefer France to America ;
he was preffed to go there, which he never was
to come here ; there he could have done no
harm, here he may. If he had went to his a-
dopted country, and accompanied his colleague,

---

* When we reflect on the degradation of this quondam Le-
giflator, it is fome confolation that he is an Englifhman.

Paine, in his legiflative career, he might have
had an opportunity of *anfwering* him by word
of mouth. The bottom of a dungeon would
have been a very fit place for them to debate,
like Milton's fallen Angels, on the fureft means
of fowing difcord among mankind, and fedu-
cing them from their Maker.

One obfervation more on this *anfwer* to Paine,
and I difmifs it for ever.

The zealous *anfwerer* boafts of his freedom as
an *American* at the fame time that he calls himfelf a *citizen of France* and a Fellow of the *Royal*
fociety of London! This is being literally,
" all things to all men." With the Englifh he is
a *Royalift*, with the Americans, a *Republican*,
and with the French, a *Carmagnole*. Thus the
triple Goddefs (under whofe influence, Doctor
Harrington fwears, he acts) is called *Luna* in
heaven, *Diana* on earth, and *Hecate* in Hell.

Before I bid the Doctor adieu, I fhould be glad
to afk him how he finds himfelf in his " *afylum*."
It is faid, he has declared that the duplicity of
our Land-Jobbers is more to be feared than the
outrages of a Birmingham Mob; and, indeed, if
all his complaints had had the fame appearance
of being well founded, the public would never
have been troubled with thefe obfervations; for,
there is little doubt of his having been moft
cruelly fleeced. This honeft profeffion, vulgarly
called land-jobbing, a member of Congrefs very
juftly ftyled " fwindling upon a broad fcale;"
it is, in fact, a South-Sea bubble upon *terra firma*,
as hundreds and thoufands of ruined foreigners, befides Doctor Prieftley, can teftify.

It is to be hoped that the Doctor's anger against his country is by this time nearly assuaged: dear bought experience has at last taught him, that an Utopia never existed any where but in a delirious brain. He thought, like too many others, to find America a Terrestrial Paradise; a Land of Canaan, where he would have nothing to do, but open his mouth and swallow the milk and honey: but, alas! he is now convinced, I believe, that those who cultivate the fertile Lesowes of Warwickshire,

" Where all around the gentlest breezes play
" Where gentle music melts on every spray,

have little reason to envy him his rocks and his swamps, the music of his bull frogs and the stings of his musquitos.

In the preface, so often mentioned, the Doctor expresses a desire of one day returning to " the land that gave him birth; " and, no offence to the New-York addressers, I think we ought to wish that this desire may be very soon accomplished. He is a bird of passage that has visited us, only to avoid the rigour of an inclement season: when the re-animating sunshine of revolution shall burst forth on his native clime, we may hope to see him prune his wings, and take his flight from the dreary banks of the Susquehannah to those of the Thames or the Avon.

L

THE

SHORT but COMPREHENSIVE

STORY

OF

A FARMER's BULL.

———————

A CERTAIN troublefome fellow, who turned his back upon the church, having occafion
to pafs through a large farm-yard in his way to
Meeting-houfe, met with a fine majeftic venerable
old Bull, lying down at his eafe, and bafking in
the fun-fhine. This Bull was at times the tameft
creature in the world ; he would fuffer the
curs to yelp at him, the flies to teafe him, and
even fome of the mifchievous fellows to pull
him by the horns. He was at this very moment
in one of his gentleft humours ; ruminating
upon paft and prefent fcenes of delight ; con-
templating the neighbouring dairy and the
farm-yard, where the milch cows had all their
bags diftended till they were nearly running
over ; the calves, and the pigs, and the poultry,
were frifking, and grunting, and crowing on ev-

ery dung-hill ; the granaries were full, and the barns ready to burſt : there were, beſides, many a goodly rick of wheat, and barley, and oats, and peaſe, and beans, and hay, and rye-graſs and clover. The dairy was full of curds, and cream, and butter, and cheeſe of every kind. To be ſure, there was plenty for the maſter and his family, and all the ſervants, and every body belonging to the farm. Nay, thoſe that were poor and needy, and idle, and lazy, and ſick, and proud, and ſaucy, and old, and infirm, and ſilly, were freely ſupplied : and even this troubleſome fellow himſelf, notwithſtanding he had long ſince quarrelled with the head-farmer and all his beſt friends, and an old grudge was ſtill ſubſiſting betwixt them, yet, upon making at any time a ſolemn promiſe to do no miſchief, had free ingreſs, egreſs, and regreſs, into every part of the farm and the dairy, and was at liberty to help himſelf wherever he liked. In ſhort he was allowed to do any thing but *ſkim the cream* and ſet *his own mark upon the butter.*

Now, becauſe the bull had happened to place himſelf acroſs his favourite foot-path, although there was plenty of room to the right and to the left, nothing would ſatisfy this impudent fellow, but he muſt kick *Old John,* for that was the Bull's name, out of his way : and all the world agrees that *John* ſuffered him to kick a long while, before he ſhewed the leaſt inclination to riſe and reſent the affront. At laſt, however he got upon his legs, and began to look round him, but ſtill it was a look of contempt only, which the fooliſh fellow miſtook for the marks of fear ;

and now, growing bolder and bolder, and hal-
looing the curs, and calling all his comrades to
prick and goad him in the tendereft paits of his
body, the Bull began to threaten and roar; —
this was on the 14th of July, one of the hotteft
days in the fummer, when fome body threw a
fiery ftick under his tail, at the very moment that
a parcel of impudent half witted fellows were
trying to flourifh a French flambeau (lighted
and blazing at both ends) full in his face. —
No wonder that the Bull fhould fet off with a
vengeance into the ftreet : — down went the
gingerbread-ftalls, and the hard-ware fhops, the
buckle menders and the razor-grinders, and the
dagger-makers : he even got into private houfes,
and in one place threw down whole bafkets full
of bottles and chemical glaffes, crucibles and
gun-barrels ; — fmafh went all the jars of inflammable air, which inftantly took fire, and
fpread all over the place; every thing went to
rack and ruin ; nothing was fafe ; even the religious houfes themfelves, where nothing had
ever been heard but the moft pious exhortations
(like thofe of Doctor Viceffimus Knox), to peace
and harmony, and obedience to the governing
powers. In fhort, nothing could pacify, or put
a ftop to, the fury of this poor enraged animal,
till his honeft mafter the farmer, as quiet and as
good a kind of church-going man as ever lived
in the world, father of a large family, hearing
of the rumpus, fent a number of his beft and
fteadieft old fervants to muzzle the beaft, which
had already toffed the fellow with the fiery ftick
over the tops of the houfes, and gored him in
fifty different places. It was next to a miracle that

he efcaped with his life; and every body thought he had reafon to be thankful that he got off fo well as he did ; but no fooner did he find himfelf fafe in a *Hackney*-coach, than, to the aftonifhment of all the world, he began to *preach* up his innocence and to lodge a complaint againft poor *Old John*, who, in the end, fuffered a great deal more than himfelf. Some filly people pitied him ; fome laughed at him ; others again were wicked enough to wifh him at the devil : — even his beft friends were afhamed of him ; and although they, one and all, defended him as much as they could in public, there was a confounded deal of muttering and grumbling in private. " I thought what it would come to," faid one ; " a pretty method of driving a mad Bull through the church-pales, " faid another.

But, to go on with my ftory ; no fooner was the Bull fairly muzzled, and properly confined, than the friends and neighbours on both fides were called in, to enquire into the whole affair; but there were fo many contradictory ftories, that it was impoffible to come at the truth, how it happened, or who had firft provoked him ; but fince it was plain to every body that *Old John* did the mifchief, and as he was proved to be the Town Bull, it was at laft fettled that the parifh fhould pay all the damages, for not keeping him in better order.

And here again was frefh matter for difcontent : fome thought it hard to pay for all the inflammable air, which had done full as much mifchief as the Bull. Others again objected to a monftrous out-of-the-way heavy demand for a large quantity (feveral reams) of fools-cap pa-

per, which had been fcribbled upon and fpoiled
long before the affair happened. Indeed, in the
opinion of fome fenfible perfons, it was fit
for nothing but kindling the fire.

But the ftrangeft part of the ftory remains to
be told ; for when this buftle was all over and
fettled, and every body thought the perverfe fellow was going to take to his church, and get
his living in an honeft way, what did he do but
fet to work bottling up his own f-rts, and felling
them for fuperfine inflammable air, and what's ftill
worfe, had the impudence to want a patent for the
difcovery ; and, indeed, a good many people were
deceived for a long time; but, they fay, two of a
trade can never agree, and fo it happened here; for
a brother trade one day catched him at his dirty
tricks and expofed him to the whole parifh. After
this all the neighbours cried fhame on him : the
women laughed, the girls they tittered, even the
little boys pointed at him and made game of him
as he went along the ftreet. In fhort, one dark
night when all the neighbourhood was quiet and
every body faft afleep, up he got and fat off into
into the next parifh, bag and baggage.

Here he trumped up a terrible ftory, pretended to be frightened to death, and fwore and
d——d his foul if the Bull was not juft at his
heels. The good folks (who, by the by, had a
monftrous grudge againft *Old John*) believed
him at once : and now there was the devil to
do again ; the women fcreamed and fell into fits ;
out run the men and boys with broomfticks and
pitchforks and fcalping knives to kill the Bull :
but it was all a fham, for poor *Old John* was
quiet at home, grazing in the meadow, up to

his eyes in clover, and blue-bells, and daffodils, and cows-lips, and primrofes, as contented as a lamb, and neither thinking nor caring any more about the fellow with the fiery ftick than about one of the flies that he was brufhing off with his tail.

But the worft of all is to come yet; for while thefe filly people were running about and making a hue and cry againft *Old John*, their *own Bull* (a thirfty beaft that they had penned up in a barren lot, without any pond or water-ing-place) broke loofe, and did ten times more mifchief than *John* had ever done. This made a fine laugh all round the country; every body faid it ferved them juft right; and fo be fure it did, for they fhould have looked at home, and minded their own Bull, and not run bawling about after *Old John*.

F I N I S.

www.ingramcontent.com/pod-product-compliance
Lightning Source LLC
Chambersburg PA
CBHW020046030726
47499CB00007B/2616